Overexposed

The Queen's Wayfarers
Book 1

by

Bill Palmer
"Lightmancer"

Overexposed

The Queen's Wayfarers Book 1

ISBN: 978-1-78808-572-4

First published in 2017

Original text © Bill Palmer 2017

All rights reserved. No part of this publication may be reproduced, stored in a retrieval system or transmitted in any form or by any means – electronic, photocopying, recording or otherwise – without the express written permission of the author having been obtained beforehand.

This book may not be sold, resold, hired out or otherwise disposed of by way of trade in any form of binding or cover other than that in which it is published, without the prior consent of the author.

This book is a work of fiction and, except in the case of historical fact, any resemblance to actual persons, living or dead, is purely coincidental.

Table of Contents

Foreword 5

Chapter 1 15
Chapter 2 22
Chapter 3 29
Chapter 4 45
Chapter 5 52
Chapter 6 59
Chapter 7 66
Chapter 8 73
Chapter 9 84
Chapter 10 88
Chapter 11 94
Chapter 12 99
Chapter 13 106
Chapter 14 113
Chapter 15 118
Chapter 16 123
Chapter 17 132
Chapter 18 141
Chapter 19 148
Chapter 20 162
Chapter 21 171
Chapter 22 189
Chapter 23 204
Chapter 24 214
Chapter 25 224
Chapter 26 231
Chapter 27 243
Chapter 28 254
Chapter 29 264
Chapter 30 269
Chapter 31 278
Chapter 32 287
Chapter 33 298
Chapter 34 309
Afterword 314

What's real – and what isn't – probably... 320
Acknowledgements 322
About the Author 323

This book is dedicated to James, or as he describes himself, me with upgrades.

Proud of you, Son.

"Travelling – it leaves you speechless then turns you into a storyteller..."
Ibn Battuta

Foreword

As they ascended in the lift the noises of the reception still in full swing in the ballroom faded to a soft murmur, then nothing. An accentless female voice announced their arrival at the third floor. She stepped out of the lift first and stood for an instant looking to left and right down the long corridors before beckoning him forward. Both ends of the corridor were in darkness thanks to the energy-efficient motion-sensitive lights, but she seemed to be able to see in the dark.

She strode along the corridor and the lights in front of her brightened as she walked. He flashed a brief smile and followed. It felt like she was lighting his way. He lengthened his stride to catch her up and undid his bow tie as he walked; it was a relief to be able to breathe again. He weaved slightly and reached out a hand to the wall to steady himself - he wasn't used to so much single malt in one evening. She stopped at the door to the Spirit Suite and held out her hand. He stared uncomprehending for a heartbeat then realised and started pocket-patting. With a sigh she reached over and took his keycard from the breast pocket of his dinner jacket. In a fluid motion she slipped it into the slot and opened the door, leading the way inside, flipping on the lights as she did so. After a moment he followed.

She walked swiftly from lounge to bedroom and finally the bathroom, giving each a swift check.

Satisfied, she returned and shrugged off her dove grey leather jacket.

The SIG Sauer in the tactical shoulder harness was incongruous against her pale satin blouse and he wondered for a moment if it was uncomfortable. It must have been because she shrugged her way out of it and dropped it onto the glass coffee table beside her jacket. He watched as she stood for a moment and massaged and flexed her shoulder. Then she looked at him and he felt himself redden; he hoped she had not caught the expression on his face.

'Sir, I have reason to believe that you are pissed. I would be derelict in my duty if I didn't take steps to sober you up before I leave you for the night.' She crossed to the Nespresso coffee machine and studied the capsules in the holder before selecting a robust espresso. It took a moment to work the machine and she turned to hand him the small cup and saucer. He had slipped out of his own jacket and launched it across the room; it hit the leather armchair and slithered to the floor.

She raised an eyebrow. 'Smooth. Not. ...Sir.' He took the cup and made his way to the sofa.

'Have one yourself. I hate to drink alone - even coffee.'

She smiled and stood for a moment lost in thought.

He couldn't help but notice the slight pout of her lips as she did so.

It was as if she was struggling with an inner dilemma.

'I will - but I don't drink coffee.' She glanced back at the cabinet. 'But... I have seen you back to your room so I am now technically off-duty; may I raid the minibar?'

He took a sip of the strong, bitter coffee and nodded. 'Of course, ah... what would you like?'

She crossed the room again. He couldn't help but notice the feline grace of her movements as she bent to look into the minibar. He knew he was a little drunk but he wasn't blind - or stupid.

'Nothing as good as what you were drinking downstairs, but...' She cracked the seal on a miniature bottle of Glenmorangie and poured all the contents into a tumbler. She swirled the whisky around the glass and inhaled deeply, letting the smoky aroma fill her nostrils. She tossed back her head and absently pulled a strand of hair back from her face; it had escaped from her neat ponytail - he had noticed it earlier.

'Ice? Water?'

'Neither... Thank you. My father brought me up to take it neat.'

She took a deep swig and held it in her mouth for a moment, before swallowing. That pout again. He tried to look away but found himself staring - again.

She breathed deeply and lowered the glass.

'Better?'

'Infinitely - thank you. Long day. You are not the easiest man to shadow - Sir.'

He grinned and tapped the seat beside him. 'Take the weight off your feet then - just while you drink your Scotch.'

She rounded the glass table, putting her tumbler down on it as she did so with a faint clink. He edged over to make room for her and watched as she flipped out one of the cushions and perched herself on the edge of the seat, hands on her knees and feet tightly together as if at an interview.

'Okay... Just for a moment.'

'A moment. Yes. That's all. You can relax you know; you said yourself you were off duty now.' The words sounded fine in his head... he hoped they made sense when he actually said them out loud.

Gingerly she leaned back against the arm of the sofa.

She looked, he thought, like a gazelle trying to make itself comfortable in a lion's den. She flicked at the errant strand of hair again and reached for her glass.

They sat for a moment in silence. She put her glass down once more - almost empty already, he noted absently - then took a deep breath, kicked off her shoes and curled her legs underneath her. The act raised her up slightly and she caught her shoulder on the lamp that was standing beside the sofa. It rocked and swayed on it's heavy base and came to rest again spotlighting her like a theatre keylight. She squinted and blinked.

'It's in your eyes. Here, let me... ' He tucked one of his own legs under himself as he leaned across to flip the light switch. At the same moment she reached again for her glass and they bumped awkwardly against each other. A drop of Glenmorangie escaped and splashed across her fingers. He apologised profusely and watched as she shook her hand then put two fingers into her mouth.

'It was nothing.' She said, her words muffled by her fingers.

'Pardon?'

She took her fingers from her lips and spoke again. 'It was nothing. Don't…'

As she spoke, he leaned close once more and took her hand in his. She didn't resist as he took her fingers into his own mouth and sucked them, slowly and gently. He looked into her eyes as he did so, suddenly very aware of what he was doing - aware, and very much alive. She sat frozen for a few seconds, until he paused. He kissed the tips of her fingers and released her hand.

'Shame to waste a decent whisky...'

For a heartbeat neither moved. His heart pounded as he tried desperately to work out whether he had misread the situation - overstepped the mark. She was younger than him, by far. She had no reason to look at him twice - but... She gazed at the glass on the table for what felt like a lifetime then reached across and dipped her fingers into the dregs at the bottom of the glass.

She held them out to him and a drop of Glenmorangie glistened wetly as it dripped onto the sofa. Her smile was tantalising... teasing...

'Do it again. Sir.'

He did. And more. So much more. For that one night, nothing existed beyond the cool grey walls of the Spirit Suite. Weeks of unspoken frustration and unrealised sexual tension boiled over as they came together.

Simpatico, moving their bodies to the same unheard beat, they melted into each other on the sofa then fused as one on the bed.

His energy and resilience amazed her - and her inventiveness and animal passion left him breathless. For a few short hours, stolen from two very different lives, each explored and enjoyed the other, body and soul, formal relationships forgotten, consequences ignored. The only thing that mattered to either of them in that moment was chasing the rush of complete sensual pleasure, freely given and taken.

As the first watery rays of the Sun filtered under the blackout blinds, they lay together naked and fulfilled. Sleep had been occasional and fitful, a backbeat to the complex melody of their passionate love-making. Now they were exhausted, satiated, spent. She lay close beside him on her front, her head turned away from him and cradled on one arm, her thick hair spreading across the pillow.

He ran his fingertips tenderly up and down her body and felt the goosebumps prickle her skin. His nails traced small circles on her bum cheeks and he smiled as the pressure of his palm at the base of her spine made her moan softly. He traced a path up her back once more with a firm thumb and forefinger and she arched to his touch like a cat. His questing fingers found the livid white scar by her shoulder blade and lingered for a moment.

'Did it hurt?' His mouth was dry and his voice sounded loud in his head - it had been a long time since either of them had said anything coherent to the other.

'It did. It does. It always will.'
She turned suddenly to face him, her face an unreadable mask, the pout that so fascinated him replaced by a thin line of determination. He raised a tender hand to touch her cheek but she grasped him by the wrist.

'No.'

He looked crestfallen.

'No? No, as in...'

'No as in no. Enough.' Her face softened for an instant and she gently pushed a hank of his own hair back from his face. For a moment he toyed with the thought that he probably looked right then like a middle-aged, overweight, baggy-eyed scarecrow - while the beautiful woman at his side who had just spent the night in his bed still somehow managed to look alluring. He started to speak but she put a finger on his lips.

'This was wrong. *So* wrong.' Her words tumbled out and her tone hardened with each syllable.
'Unexpected. Surprising. Wonderful. But wrong. It must stop here and no-one can ever know. Ever.'

His face fell. He started to reply, to unpack all those things that were welling up inside him that he felt he needed to say to try to reason with her, to change her mind, to somehow extend the stolen moment - but was interrupted by a persistent buzzing from his phone.

With an apologetic look he rolled upright and fished it out of his trouser pocket on the floor beside the bed and looked bleary-eyed at the text that had just come in.

"We are down to one candidate."

He rolled on his back and looked again at the woman, who returned his gaze for a heartbeat then gathered the sheet around herself and padded into to the bathroom. The door locked behind her with a click that finally punctuated their night together and snapped him back to cold reality.

He stared at the ceiling for a long time, then realised he was holding his breath. He exhaled hard then swung his feet to the floor again. From behind the closed bathroom door came the sound of a shower, washing the night away.

He picked up his phone again and after a moment of thought his thumbs flew across the screen.

'Acknowledged. Test his mettle.'

Chapter 1

Guy Miller stood, stretched and moved toward the doors as his train neared Waterloo. After 50-odd minutes in a seat from Farnham he needed to stretch his legs before walking up the platform. At 50 years of age he wasn't exactly unfit but standing at 6'2" in his socks he found South West Trains in rush hour a bit of a squeeze. As the train slowed on its final approach he ran through his mental checklist. A hand absently patted the Billingham Hadley Pro slung from his left shoulder.

Inside was his Fuji X-Pro2 fitted with a 35mm lens. In the compartment alongside was a 23mm and a 50mm Zeiss. His purpose that day in town was to indulge in a little street photography, ostensibly to familiarise himself with the three lens setup before his next tutorial trip in just over a fortnight, guiding half a dozen well-paying amateur photographers around the photogenic Portuguese city of Lisbon. Guy already knew the kit quite well, but it was ingrained in him to leave nothing to chance and he felt a little rusty. It was also a good chance to get together with his literary agent for a breakfast meeting and progress plans for his next book.

When he retired from the Queen's Messengers a year ago Guy had walked away from thirteen years of travelling worldwide on Her Majesty's Service. When he travelled now he had to pay his own way.

It did mean that the frequency of his trips had dropped but he had taken the time to devote himself to his long-term passion, travel photography and finally make it pay through writing a short but successful series of guide books based upon his travels and more recently the photo courses in cities like Lisbon.

Life was good, Guy mused as the train finally halted with a jerk. He and his wife Jane had a nice house on the outskirts of Farnham. She still worked part-time as a manager in a local architect's office but was easily able to get time off to accompany him on his 48-72 hour European city break "research trips".

The setup was ideal, thought Guy; as a self-employed author much of each trip was tax deductible and combined the best of both worlds - leisure and pleasure along with research for the next book or course. Jane happily left him to it on paid tutorial trips like Lisbon though - far too many "passengers" for her taste; she always said she preferred when it was just the two of them.

Guy stepped down from the train and winced involuntarily as he did so; his left knee was troubling him again, a hang-over from his days in the Royal Navy and that unfortunate incident in a fast moving RIB in the Gulf of Oman that had led to him being prematurely invalided out. He cursed himself for leading with his left, resolved to take it to the doctor once more after Lisbon and hobbled to the entrance to the Tube.

Breakfast was pleasant as always, this time in an All Bar One at Butler's Wharf, close to Tower Bridge. His agent was late as usual and it was past 11 when they parted, with the good news that his first two books were to be reprinted once more and that the third had definitely been green-lit for an Autumn publication, together with a promise of a US release and - best of all - a reasonably generous advance. His agent uncharacteristically picked up the bill so perhaps he had felt just a little guilty for being late.

Guy walked across Tower Bridge with a spring in his step, camera in hand and the streets around Spitalfields as a destination in mind. He was in his element, tripping the shutter gently and frequently as he strolled, capturing the life of London in the early Spring. He barely formed conscious thoughts as he went with the flow of the people around him and settled into the rhythm of the city.

The shadows were beginning to lengthen as Guy stood in front of a wall full of particularly photogenic graffiti on the corner of Bell Lane, swapping lenses. It was a well-practiced manoeuvre for him; he held the both the 23 and the 35 still on the camera front element to front element, in his left hand and released the 35 from the X-Pro with a deft flick of his right index finger.

A quarter turn and then a 180-degree rotation of his left wrist removed one lens from the camera and offered up the other in its place.

A last quarter turn and the change was made; it took far longer to describe than to do. As he recapped the 35 and dropped it back into the depths of the Billingham he heard the voice behind him.

"Nice camera…"

Guy tensed. In his experience there were only two kinds of people who commented out of the blue on his kit. They could be broadly summed up as either "inquisitive" or "acquisitive". The former was harmless... often another photographer with a genuine curiosity about the camera or lens he was using. You met them, occasionally, when shooting street. They ranged from harmless to entertaining.

The latter was more of an issue. He turned slowly to see that he was dealing with an example of same. Before him stood a man in his early thirties, unshaven, unkempt and apparently unloved. A grimy black leather jacket with a large tear under one armpit covered a thick sweater that had once been red but now was tainted by stains that it probably didn't do to examine too closely. The stains, Guy mused, probably accounted for at least thirty per cent of the odours that now washed over him. The remaining seventy per cent were apparently directly attributable to poor personal hygiene.

Guy tended not to worry too much about his personal safety while taking photos; he was more than capable of looking out for himself.

His basic training while in the Navy had been augmented by his all too short stint in the Special Boat Service. He was one of the few regular Royal Navy officers to have been accepted into the elite force and had enjoyed it – up to the point at which his knee got in the way.

'Lovely day.' Said Guy conversationally. He adopted an expression of genuine concern and took a half step toward the man.

'How long has it been since you spoke to your mum? Is she feeling better these days?'

The combination of unexpected personal question and moving directly into the man's personal space created immediate cognitive dissonance, exactly as Guy intended. It was a highly effective ploy and one that he had used more than once in the past. Often petty street crime was born of desperation and was out of character as a result. Guy knew that if he could break his interrogators concentration for just a second or two he could use that time to move out of the immediate danger zone.

But not this time.

The man shook his head as if clearing his thoughts and stuck out his hand. Guy experienced a slight dissonance of his own as he noticed that the grubby fingers protruding from the woolly mitt on the man's hand were surprisingly well manicured.

That wasn't important right now.

He had just moved himself in Guy's mind from irritant to open threat and was now presenting enough of a problem to warrant direct action - no more mind-games, this situation had passed beyond his ability to defuse with words.

Twenty-odd years ago, even ten, Guy would have dealt with the attempted mugger quickly and efficiently, with a minimum of fuss or risk. He would have been taller, faster, better trained and fitter. Now he could just about still count on better trained – and of course taller.

And wily. Don't forget wily…

Guy's shoulders slumped slightly as he accepted the situation. 'Bugger…' he muttered under his breath and started to fumble with the X-Pro2 in his hand. 'Okay, look, just let me take out the SD card, right? It's of no value to you but there's pictures of my family on it...'

He held the camera low, in his right hand, pointing to it with his left. His would-be assailant took a step forward, eyes focussed on the prize that would soon be his - he had the air of a man who knew a man who might even give him thirty quid for it…

Guy's hand moved up in a short arc and drove the hard edge of the camera body straight into the mugger's face.

He felt rather than heard the crunch of cartilage and bone as a kilo and a bit of solid camera met the bridge of the man's nose. Guy accentuated the effect by following through, using momentum and his body weight to force his assailant upright and over, until he overbalanced and flopped down hard onto his back. His old Krav Maga instructor would have been proud.

Breathing hard as much from the spike of adrenaline as the exertion, Guy turned and ran as quickly as his knee would let him back towards the main road, people and relative safety.

Had he turned to look back he would have seen his assailant scramble back to his feet, spitting and snorting blood and trying to catch his breath. After a minute or so he felt well enough to pull a small walkie-talkie from an inside pocket.

'Red Queen, this is White Rabbit. Subject passed reaction test with honours. He's all yours, Beth...' He spat blood again '...request pickup. And get me to a fucking doctor.'

Chapter 2

Guy sat in a pub with a large Jamesons in front of him. He'd contemplated for a nanosecond reporting the incident to the police, but then decided against it - they surely had better things to do than to investigate a failed robbery by a down-on-his-luck vagrant. He was fine, and his camera had survived unscathed, albeit a little bloodstained. Fortunately it was weather-resistant so that would clean off in due course. It sat in front of him now.

'What are you looking at?' he muttered. 'I just saved you from a fate worse than death.' Inwardly he cursed himself. He had allowed his instincts and adrenaline to take over. He could have handed the camera over - it was insured - but it simply wasn't in his nature to be pushed around. 'Stupid, stupid, stupid' he chanted under his breath for the fourth or fifth time. He wasn't getting any younger and his wife wouldn't thank him for getting himself hospitalised. Now his knee ached, his feet were sore and his hands had only just stopped shaking.

Guy was so engrossed in his own thoughts at that moment that he failed to notice the smartly dressed man and woman who had slid onto the bar stools to his right and left. They exchanged glances behind his back then the man spoke.

'Mr. Miller. May we have a word?' Guy turned to find a warrant card in his eye-line for an instant.

It disappeared again before he could make out any detail.

'We have reason to believe you were involved in an assault earlier this afternoon.' The woman, now behind him, spoke for the first time. Guy's head snapped around like a cartoon character at the sound of her voice; there was a Welsh lilt there that was not unattractive. Her own warrant card was similarly flashed and stashed before he could read any more than her name and rank. Detective Sergeant. Owen.

His head snapped around again. The man was standing already and had picked up his Fuji from the bar. He turned it in his hands and studied the traces of blood with a slight nod to his partner. She was on her feet now too, his tan Billingham slung awkwardly over the shoulder of her dark trouser suit.

Guy regained a modicum of his composure; things were moving too damn fast for his taste, and didn't feel right. 'Is this an arrest? Surely PACE requires that you tell me my rights.'

'No, Mr. Miller you are not being arrested. We are just taking you to see someone who would like a conversation with you.' The man took him by the elbow with a firm but not quite painful grip - he was stronger than he looked - and started to propel him toward the door.

Guy was herded into a black Ford Galaxy that was waiting just outside the pub door. Owen sat beside him and the male officer up front beside the driver. Neither said a word and Guy's attempts to strike up a conversation were met with a stony silence. He fell quiet and watched the world go by through the smoked glass.

He sat up straighter when after a few minutes drive he realised that they were circumnavigating Parliament Square. He raised an eyebrow when they turned into a nondescript entrance that took them to a subterranean parking facility under the Palace of Westminster itself.

The Ford descended some ramps then came to a halt by an unobtrusive set of lift doors at the rear of the car park. The door opened and Guy was ushered out. The male officer stayed aboard, but Owen accompanied him, his bag still slung over her shoulder.

She pushed the call button for the lift and the doors opened immediately. They stepped inside and she typed in a series of digits on a numeric keypad.

The doors shut and Guy lost his balance for a moment when the lift unexpectedly started to descend. He shot a quizzical glance at Owen and saw a twinkle in her eye.

'You weren't expecting that...' She smiled for the first time.

'No shit. How far…'

He was interrupted by a soft ping as the doors opened. A thoroughly normal, modern office reception desk stood in a spacious white room equipped with visitor chairs, bottled water and a coffee machine. The only thing missing was windows although a slightly faded mural of the Thames across one wall provided some eye relief.

The receptionist was expecting them. Owen had already pulled from her pocket an identification badge which she put around her neck on a lanyard and Guy was handed something similar. He studied the pass in his hand. It was white, plain except for a day-glo orange crown with the words "accompanied visitor" beneath it in large friendly letters.

'This way Mr. Miller.' Owen led the way along a short corridor, past several glass-walled conference rooms before opening the door to one. A man inside rose to his feet as they entered. Owen left, closing the door soundlessly behind her.

Guy turned quickly and laid a hand on the door handle and tugged hard. 'Just a minute - she has my bag!' The door did not budge.

The man behind him spoke for the first time. 'Sit down, please, Guy. Detective Sergeant Owen is quite trustworthy. She will ensure that your belongings are safe and that the, um, unfortunate marks are removed. Everything will be returned to you in good order when you leave. I may call you Guy, I trust?'

'No you may not. Who are you? What do you want? Where am I?'

The man smiled thinly. 'I shall call you "Mr. Miller" for now, I think, at least until I have earned a little of your trust. My name is Roger Bowman. You are here because I am interested in you.' He laid an iPad on the table in front of him and flicked rapidly through a number of screens of text and pictures as if refreshing his memory. Even upside-down Guy could see that it was a file of information about him.

'You are not my type, Bowman. If I am not actually under arrest I want to leave - now.'

'No, Mr. Miller, you don't. You are curious by nature and you are consumed right now with a desire to know why you have been brought here.' He sat and indicated a chair. Guy warily lowered himself into it.

Bowman picked up the iPad and began to read aloud. 'Guy Miller, ex-Royal Navy, rose to the rank of Lieutenant before applying to join the SBS.

You were accepted and completed basic training before sustaining an injury to your knee on your first mission in 2001 that led to your being invalided out.

After a year of drifting and feeling sorry for yourself your ex-CO intervened and referred you to become a Queen's Messenger.

You served as such with distinction for 13 years until taking early retirement. You now fill your time as a freelance author and photography tutor. You have been happily married for twenty-six years, with two - no, three - grown up children. Mortgage-free, no debt to speak of, save a small loan outstanding on your wife's car, which you could easily clear from your savings.' He paused for breath.

'I suppose you are going to tell me my inside leg measurement too.'

'I could. I believe we have a record of your tailor somewhere in the appendices. You have, ah - expanded – slightly over the years, I seem to recall. Still, none of us are the shape we were in our twenties, eh?'

Guy was ready to explode. 'Who - or what - the Hell are you, Bowman? How dare you go sniffing around my life like this. It's completely unacceptable.'

'Yes, Mr. Miller, I can see how you might think that, but let me assure you that it is completely justified and entirely necessary. You will be pleased to know that you have a clean record, at least for our purposes.

You passed your final hurdle this afternoon when you, ah… neutralised - your assailant in Spitalfields. I am sure you will be relieved to learn that our Mr Romano has now received medical treatment to his nose and should suffer no lasting effects beyond an increased propensity to snore.'

Guy gaped open-mouthed at Bowman, who switched off the iPad and laid it on the table in front of him. 'That was a *test*? What sort of nutter are you?'

'A determined and deadly serious one, Mr. Miller. Let me be blunt. Your country needs you. If you want to know for what, and why, I suggest you walk with me.'

Bowman stood abruptly, gathered up the iPad and walked to the door. It opened easily to his touch. Guy sat for a moment in stunned silence then rose to follow.

Chapter 3

Bowman led the way through a nondescript door and along an oak-panelled corridor to a set of imposing double doors at one end. Portraits of men and women in period costume stared down. After a few paces Guy noticed that each portrait, although different in style, subject and era had one thing in common - a stylised compass rose surmounted by a crown appeared in the upper right of each painting.

No - wait - there was a difference. Some had four points, some eight, or sixteen. In each case one point was picked out in a different colour. The point thus highlighted varied from one painting to the next. Nearing the doors, Guy was about to ask Bowman about it when he suddenly realised that he recognised one of the subjects.

'That's Alan Whicker!' he said in surprise. 'Why on Earth do you have a portrait of Alan Whicker all the way down here?' Bowman nodded, and pointed at a couple of other portraits.

'It is indeed. And that is Eric Newby. That one over there - Patrick Leigh Fermor...'

He stopped in front of the double doors and grasped the ornate doorhandles with both hands. To Guy's further surprise he let go again after a second and took half a step back as the doors soundlessly swung outwards.

'We do get some lovely toys' he said conversationally. 'These door handles conduct a biometric scan when touched. They don't only make sure that I'm me and that my hands are attached -' Guy raised an eyebrow at that '- but also that I am not unduly stressed, which might indicate coercion. It's not foolproof, unfortunately - it can't differentiate between a bad journey in on the Jubilee Line or a gun to my head, but better to be safe than sorry, eh? Tea?'

Guy nodded absently. His attention was absorbed by the contents of the room.

Bowman busied himself at a small sideboard that prosaically held a small chrome Swan kettle and a china teapot together with cups, saucers and a caddy of different teas.

'Earl Grey, your file says?' Guy nodded again, wondering at the level of detail held on him. He resolved to cut up his Waitrose loyalty card later.

He stepped forward into the pool of light in the centre of the circular chamber. It was clearly set up as some sort of conference room, with more oak panelled walls and a large, highly polished circular table in the middle, which Guy realised as he approached was actually made up of a set of smaller segments, sixteen in all. A single gap in the sweep of the tables faced the door they had entered by and allowed access to the exact centre of both the room and the table.

It was a void, but it was not empty.

Spinning dead-centre was a globe, roughly ten feet in diameter. It had no visible means of support as it turned slowly some three feet above the marble floor. Oddly it left no shadow but instead cast a pale light of its own. Guy walked closer and waved a hand through India and Sri Lanka. The globe shivered slightly but was otherwise undisturbed.

'Hologram' said Bowman, handing him a teacup and saucer. A chocolate Bourbon biscuit rested on the edge. 'The globe used to be analogue - a bloody great thing, all ebony and ivory. Pain in the arse. Juddered sometimes when it turned. Apparently the Victorians inlaid pink coral all over it to show the extent of the Empire but that threw the whole thing out of balance and it ate ball bearings for decades after that. This is much better. 4K, 3D, zoom, surround sound, and it doesn't even need dusting. Take a seat.'

He gestured for Guy to step out of the centre first and closed a flap behind them to complete the circle.

Guy smiled at the resolutely low-tech nature of the action after the whizzy doorhandles and globe - a bit like the bar at the Rose and Crown... Bowman led the way, walking all the way around to a chair directly opposite the door.

Guy settled himself at the next nearest seat.
He realised that in the whole room there were only eight chairs including the ones that he and Bowman currently occupied.

The segment of table in front of Bowman had a large but subtle inlay, almost the same colour as the desktop itself. By tilting his head slightly and letting the light from the globe play across it Guy made out a large capital "N".

Bowman took a sip of his own tea and settled back in his chair. 'Explanation time.' He began. 'How's your English history - specifically the Elizabethan era?'

'Raleigh, Drake, Hawkins, Shakespeare, New World, potatoes, tobacco, the Spanish Armada, Dr. John Dee, Mary Queen of Scots, that sort of thing? I'm fuzzy on the details and who did what to whom.'

'You've already demonstrated you know more than 90 per cent of the population. Have you ever heard of Francis Walsingham? The Queen's Intelligencer?'

'No…?'

He was Elizabeth the First's Chief Spymaster. An honest to goodness, real life M, long before Fleming was born, let alone invented Commander Bond. The Elizabethans in fact brought espionage to a fine art. Spies have been around for ever, of course - the second oldest profession - but Walsingham raised England's game and in so doing helped put the realm on the path to greater things.'
'So this -' Guy waved his arm '- is all part of some super secret spy thing? Oh come *on*…'

Bowman grimaced. 'Nothing so sordid, Mr. Miller. We leave all that grubby stuff to the boys and girls up the river.' He pondered for a moment and took another sip of his tea.

'Shall we approach this from a different direction? Let's think for a moment about what you did when you were a Queen's Messenger. For years you carried the "diplomatic bag" - dispatches and materials to and from British embassies worldwide. It's an old and honourable role, of course; books have been written about it. You had a diplomatic passport to go with your status. By convention and treaty diplomatic couriers may pass national borders without let or hindrance, may they not?'

Guy shrugged dismissively. 'You clearly already know all this already - what's your point?'

'Did you ever wonder what you *actually* carried? Did you ever ponder the …legality of it?'

'Of course. Mostly it was just papers – dispatches. Sometimes it was money, large amounts in high denomination notes. Bottles of good single malt were not unknown, particularly at Christmas.

But we all knew that we sometimes carried "sensitive" items. There were times when I knew that the attaché case on the plane seat at my side contained two Browning HPs and enough ammunition to rob a bank. In fact I can think of more than one occasion where bank robberies coincidentally occurred not long after I had boarded a flight home.'

'Indeed. And a small amount of cash was reported stolen, but the disappearance of a safe deposit box or two was largely ignored by the media. And then a few months later a politician was disgraced, a popular movement destabilised, a government won - or lost - an election against the odds…'

Guy shrugged non-committally. 'I'm sure I know nothing about such matters. Pure coincidence. These things happen all the time.'

'Yes, indeed they do. And sometimes, I'm assured, they even happen of their own accord. But more often than not, circumstances are gently nudged by one player or another in one direction or another; coincidence is given, ah, a hand.'

Guy shifted impatiently in his chair. The resultant squeak echoed loudly in the large room and irritated him further.

'Get to the point, Bowman. Are you recruiting spies or not? If you are I am really not interested.'

Bowman waved a hand in mock surrender.

'I can see that patience is not your strong suit. Back to the plot. Walsingham created an unrivalled network of loyal spies who were embedded in the royal courts and parliaments of England's enemies - and friends.

He took time - sometimes years on end - to ensure that they were above all suspicion – completely beyond reproach.

It would be impossible for those same spies to suddenly drop everything, hop across the Channel and deliver their reports to The Crown in person without arousing suspicion – so, a network of couriers was established to service them.

These courageous men and women were not themselves spies, in the true sense of the word in that they did not themselves conduct intelligence gathering or, ah, espionage, but the information that they carried to and fro was by definition of such sensitivity that if it had been exposed to public scrutiny it could have had serious ramifications up to and including constituting a threat to the very existence of The Crown and the realm itself.

Walsingham was no fool and was an early believer in the power of "hiding in plain sight".

He employed as his couriers men and women who were already known to travel, often extensively, by the nature of what they did – merchants, traders, actors, scientists, clerics, artists, authors, et cetera. No eyebrow was raised by their criss-crossing national borders.

They concealed their true intent by being open and obvious in their presence and movements. Some were regarded as eccentrics, deliberately drawing considerable attention to themselves. Some had already achieved fame - or notoriety - before themselves being recruited. All had certain -' He coughed and took another sip of tea '- attributes. They were experienced, skilled, mature and resourceful. Men and women of the world, you may say.

Whicker is a grand example. Ex-military, unflappable, affable, well travelled and yet at home in absolutely any environment. Think of the places he went, the people he met. Remember that interview with Papa Doc Duvalier in Haiti? Do you think that just happened? He had one of the longest careers of any of us. In fact he was a predecessor of mine in this very seat.

Guy was intrigued now. His brain raced.

'Eric Newby? Even him? You pointed out his painting on the wall.'

'Yes, even him. You don't think he went for "A short walk in the Hindu Kush" just to take the mountain air, do you?'

'Good grief - so - Michael Palin... "Pole to Pole". Wasn't he filming in Russia just weeks before the fall of the Soviet Union…?'

Bowman shrugged. 'Indeed he was, but that was just one of those coincidences of which we spoke; he's not one of ours.'

Bowman laid a hand on the inlaid tabletop. 'Mr. Miller, we are the Queen's Wayfarers. At any one time there are a minimum of four of us.

Those four are known as 'Cardinals' after the cardinal points and between us we run the organisation on behalf of the monarch of the day.

It was Walsingham's idea - I think it amused him to take a title from the Catholic Church which was one of England's most implacable foes at the time of our foundation. I am 'North', and my three senior colleagues are 'East', 'West' and 'South' respectively. I am based here in London and the others are in Tokyo, Washington and Pretoria. Together we form the Board of Wayfarers.'

Guy leaned back with a cynical expression on his face. 'So you are a secret society within government?

Swanning around playing at Postman Pat with naughty secrets?'

Bowman looked mildly pained by the description. 'Sort of, although I wouldn't put it in quite those terms.

I would correct you on one small point though. Although we are currently under a government building that is through an accident of history; Westminster used to be a royal palace. We actually owe our charter and our allegiance to the monarch of the day. Incidentally we are always known as "The Queen's" regardless of who is actually on the throne, in honour of Elizabeth, our first patron.

By convention it is at the ruling monarch's discretion whether they inform each Prime Minister of our existence and then put us at their disposal. We were very active under Victoria, of course but her son Edward VII considered us an un-necessary luxury. A shame really. The 20th Century might have been very different had a few key messages been delivered to a few influential people before the outbreak of the Great War."

'Oh come *on*. Are you seriously trying to tell me that The Great War could have been averted if your predecessors had done a bit more scuttling around Europe before 1914?'

'No. It's not quite as simple as that. As I said already, sometimes things happen that are beyond the ability of anyone to stop or indeed to alter. Time is a living thing, Mr. Miller. It has a rhythm and a momentum all of its' own.

Make no mistake, we are simply the conduits by which information passes, not the message itself, nor what is done with it.

But, it would be true to say that when we are inactive on the World stage things do tend to happen in a less, ah, favourable... manner.

As I explained already, the incoming Prime Minister is told of our existence by the monarch of the day. It's also the case that once told some Prime Ministers have themselves chosen not to utilise our services. The last Prime Minister who did that was Blair.'

'Don't tell me - the second Gulf War...'

'Quite.'

There was silence for a long time. Bowman snapped a Rich Tea and dunked it in his cup. Guy stared at the revolving globe, deep in thought.

'Why am *I* here? - You said upstairs that you would at least answer that question.'

'Brexit.' Bowman answered, brushing biscuit crumbs absently from his lapel. 'In spite of what you have read and been told, it has been planned for, for years. The ramifications and implications have been extrapolated, analysed, understood. In the next decade and beyond, the political shape of Europe *will* transform.

Old certainties are already starting to cease to exist, treaties and alliances will crumble, national boundaries will re-assert - or in some cases not… and new, ah, alignments… will be formed.

That won't just happen at random. Forces are already at work and conversations in certain quarters are at an advanced stage, both those directly involving the UK and those that see us as a troublesome neighbour.'

'This is dynamite.' Guy said with a stony expression. 'No. It's nuclear. Perhaps literally.'

'Exactly.' Bowman nodded slowly. 'Look at Spain. How many attempts did they have at forming a stable government lately?

Meanwhile the Basques and Catalans have enjoyed local political freedoms under the aegis of the EU that they simply will not accept losing. And that is only one example.'

He jabbed a finger in the direction of the globe and it stopped abruptly, with Europe in full view. He spread his fingers and it enlarged until the landmass filled the area previously occupied by the entire world. Another gesture and familiar national boundaries shone bright. Bowman moved his hand slowly from left to right and the boundaries started to distort, fade and in some places disappear altogether. In their place new lines formed, flickering and altering hesitantly as Guy watched.

'This particular timeline projection runs to 2038. It is one of an infinite number of outcomes. It is, shall we say, one of the possible futures that is generally favourable to the realm as a whole. There are others, Far less so...'

Bowman snapped his fingers and the globe returned to normal.

'In times of great national need, Mr. Miller, the number of Queen's Wayfarers increases, to accommodate the additional, ah, supra-diplomatic "traffic". Today we are eight; the four Cardinals plus four more, but with the coming changes the dispatch volumes are already going up beyond our ability to cope in a discreet and timely manner.

In short, Mr. Miller, we are forced by circumstance to recruit once again. The maximum possible number at any one time is thirty-two - in your Royal Navy days you must have learned to "box the compass", yes?'

'Of course. "Nor', Nor' by E', Nor'-Nor' E'"and so on... That's the significance of the compass roses on the portraits, isn't it? There are 32 points on each rose...'

'Well done. I would have been disappointed if I had had to spell that little detail out for you. If I then say that this table has never seated more than 16 of us at any one time - even during global conflicts - it may help you to understand the gravity of the situation in which we find ourselves. We are currently recruiting another eight and I would very much like you to join us.'

'Bowman, I'm fifty. I'm carrying a few extra pounds. Slower than I was. I have problems with my knee...'

Bowman shrugged dismissively. ' ...and of course we won't mention the kidney stones... All unimportant. You are experienced. Worldly. You are generally able to look after yourself, and keep a cool head. You are inventive and resourceful, with a high tolerance to ambiguity. Above all you already travel regularly around Europe and beyond as part of your existing lifestyle. It won't blip on anyone's radar if one day you decide to book an Easyjet flight to Berlin, for instance.'

Guy pounced. 'Berlin? Is that where you want me to go?'

'Not this time, ah, no. We simply want you to go ahead with the itinerary of your next trip as planned, to Lisbon on Thursday of the week after next. Once you are there we would like you to collect an item - we call it a "dispatch", you know - and take it to a second rendezvous in Seville. There it will be added to – updated, you may say - and given back to you once more. All you then have to do is to return it – and yourself - safely to us here.'

'An "item"? That's more than a little vague. What is it? A letter? A dossier? Microfilm?'

'Mr. Miller, this is the 21st century. Nobody actually writes letters any more.

Equally, there is little confidence in certain quarters in the "secure" transmission of data by electronic means. Physical transport of certain above top secret information is ah, preferred.' He paused and looked pensive for a moment before he continued.

'The item in question is simply a standard Micro SD card.' 'The card you will be given in Lisbon will bear details of an agreement electronically signed by certain senior people within the Portuguese establishment. In Seville it will be electronically countersigned by like-minded people representing Spanish interests in the private and public sectors and,' he blinked once, rapidly. 'the Catholic church.'

I understand that the Spanish contribution to our little enterprise will also include a goodwill gesture – a very useful little list of French, um …"sympathisers" currently believed by our Spanish friends to be active on English soil - they are providing that as an additional proof of their own good faith. I am sure you will understand that it is vital the very existence of both the agreement itself and that list are kept in the strictest confidence.' He looked Guy in the eye.' I can trust you to do that, can't I, Mr. Miller...?'

Guy gazed at the holographic globe again then turned to face Bowman. 'You don't expect me to say no, do you, or you wouldn't be telling me all this.'

Bowman said nothing, his face impassive.

Guy sighed. 'What's the pay like? And do I get any of my own -' he indicated the holographic world with a nod '- "toys"?'

Bowman laughed for the first time. 'Civil service pay grade, a bit higher than the one you used to be on as a Queen's Messenger - oh, and it's tax-free. Toys? Don't be ridiculous. I have told you already - we are not spies - we are simply travellers for The Crown."

Chapter 4

Guy returned home late that night, far later than he had intended. Before he left, Bowman had given him a card with a number to ring with his answer. He insisted that Guy went home and talked it through with his wife before making his decision - 'We are, after all not, ah, pirates, intent on press-ganging you.' DS Owen had returned his Billingham bag to him on the way out, complete with pristine X-Pro2 and he had been given a lift in the black Galaxy back across the river to Waterloo.

Jane Miller was an intelligent and intuitive woman. In spite – or perhaps because of - his reassuring texts and warm smile (and box of Hotel Chocolat chocolates hastily purchased at Waterloo before boarding the train) when he opened the front door she knew immediately something was up.

They talked, in detail and at length, over dinner, sitting in their spacious kitchen. Jane asked a number of questions, many of which he confessed he simply didn't yet know the answer to himself. What little Guy could tell her of what he had learned of the history of the Queen's Wayfarers fascinated her and she spent a largely fruitless hour Googling the subject - to no avail.

Throughout their discussions, she kept coming back to one simple query.

'Guy, is it dangerous?'

His short and honest answer was "I don't know" but as they talked into the night his position shifted from that to "*life's* dangerous." and ended up at "How dangerous can it be?" They had been together for years, bringing up three children along the way and had got into the habit of making important life decisions together but on this occasion Jane could see that somewhere deep inside Guy's mind was already made up.

He did not - could not - tell her every detail that had been shared with him but it was clear to her that Roger Bowman had appealed to some part of Guy's character that meant her husband was already, mentally, on a journey.

In the end Jane gave him her qualified blessing, with caveats such as "Stay in touch." and "Avoid anyone who looks like Mata Hari!" They went to bed in the small hours and relieved each other's tension by the simple expedient of making love before falling asleep, entwined in each others arms.

--o-0-o--

Two weeks later Guy was on early morning Easyjet flight from Gatwick North Terminal to Lisbon. He toyed with the chewy bacon baguette in front of him and mulled over the events of the last fortnight.

His call to Bowman the next morning to say yes had triggered a chain of events. He had spent three days buried under the Palace of Westminster being given various briefings. He'd also had to complete a set of computer-based training modules - health and safety, ethics and morality - before being "certified".

A thorough medical confirmed what he knew - good basic health, bit crumbly around the edges, carrying about a stone too much weight, mostly around the middle. Arthritic knee, incipient plantar fasciitis in both feet, propensity to kidney gravel – nothing new there, and apparently not show-stoppers to his new employers. He was given a new credit card - it looked completely ordinary but he was assured that it was effectively limitless - and a block of five thousand Euros in cash. Both came with the simple instruction "Get receipts for absolutely everything." Guy sighed - some things never changed.

Bowman had been true to his word in one respect at least. Guy had not been given any sexy James Bond-esque gadgetry. The closest that they came to it was a "keyword". One word, apparently a nonsense word. It was a "Googlewhack" - a unique word with no hits at all when searched for on the internet.

Actually it was a word and a number, that amounted to the same thing if punched in on a standard numeric keypad.

The word was "threnodygild" and the equivalent number was "847366394453" both of which he was required to commit to memory. In case of dire emergency Guy could use the word - pick up a phone - any phone, and say it, or dial the number, even send it as a text.

He could also type the word or number into an ATM, or keyboard on a train ticket machine or parking machine. Anything that formed part of the "Internet of Things", Bowman assured him, was monitored by "The right people". If Guy kept the input device with him, or stayed in close proximity to it, Bowman explained, he would be located and "extracted with vigour" - a smile crossed Guy's face at the recollection of the terminology Bowman used, his face earnest.

Beyond that, it was made crystal clear that Guy was well and truly on his own. He spent time browsing the Internet and ordering a thing or two that he felt might come in handy. A further day or two was taken up with tinkering in his shed, and both he and Jane spent a lot of time researching post-Brexit politics and the implications on the global economy.

It didn't take long to establish what they already suspected - nobody really had a clear idea of what was going to happen next, but there was general agreement that the British voters had created an inflexion point in European - and World – affairs back in 2016 and that there were consequences that a great many people were not happy about.

Bowman's people had already taken it upon themselves to cancel his photography course in Lisbon, notifying the various attendees by email. Although a good cover for his being there it was thought to be for the best, Bowman explained, if he didn't have to also faff about with a dozen eager amateur snappers underfoot.

The ostensible reason of the trip therefore became reconnaissance for a future course.

This was entirely in keeping with Guy's behaviour patterns and his habit of making sure nothing was left to chance. As he said in the foreword to one of his popular photo guidebooks, "Piss Poor Planning Prevents Proper Photography". Guy was secretly glad that he had been relieved of the responsibility - it was one less thing to think of, pre-trip.

In the overhead locker above his seat was his trusty Hadley Pro, with the Fuji X-Pro2 and a brace of lenses. The Hadley in turn nestled within a nondescript backpack, which provided just enough additional room for some clothes and basic toiletries, - sufficient for a couple of days, but all still within the Easyjet hand baggage limit.

Guy detested time spent at baggage carousels and took pride in his ability to travel light when the occasion demanded, a relic of his days in the Royal Navy.

He was brought back to the present by the pilot's cheery announcement of "10 minutes to landing.".

His half-eaten baguette and empty coffee cup were whisked away and he stowed his tray table for landing. His plan on arrival was straightforward, and boringly mundane. He would pick himself up a 48-hour Lisboa Card to make travel and entrance to places easier and cheaper then grab the Aerobus 1 to take him almost to the door of his hotel, the NH Lisboa Libertade.

Once there he would dump the backpack, take another bus into town and take some photos. A Sagres beer or two in a bar near the harbour, dinner somewhere that looked friendly then back to the hotel for a night's sleep. The real purpose of his trip began the following day when he was due to meet a contact at the Castelo de São Jorge to collect the - what was the word Bowman used? "Dispatch." Guy closed his eyes and allowed his mind to drift as EZY8717 began it's final approach into the imaginatively-named Aeropuerto de Lisboa.

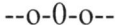

Four rows back in seat 9D a stocky, dark-haired man put down the book he had read for most of the flight and took a swig from the water bottle in his seat pocket. By leaning slightly to his left he could just see the back of Guy Miller's head. He hummed softly to himself and resumed reading. He was in no rush, and Miller would, he felt sure, would offer no real challenge to a man of his skills.

Chapter 5

Lisbon was just as Guy remembered it. Warm, relaxed, photogenic and welcoming. It was a city with a special place in his heart, since it was atop the very same Castelo de São Jorge that he had proposed on one knee to Jane, all those years ago. He made a point, whenever he visited, of going to the same spot and spending a couple of minutes there, whether Jane herself was at his side or not.

Even though he had to be at the castle tomorrow morning for the rendezvous itself he made a point of going there just after his arrival. He contented himself with a text to Jane telling her where he was, and that he missed her. He got a short response making fun of him for being an incurable romantic, but he could feel the warmth between the words.

He walked down the winding hill from the castle and found a small bar. The Sagres was ice cold and very welcome. He found himself a place at a pavement table and indulged in one of his favourite pastimes; people-watching. Well-dressed locals mingled with the first tourists and trippers of the season.

The weather could still turn quickly at this time of year and a bewildering variety of leisurewear was the result. Guy stretched out his legs, lowered his cap over his eyes and soaked in the atmosphere and the Spring sunshine.

"Allo. Do you perhaps speak English?"

Guy straightened in his seat and regarded the figure in front of him. A man in his early forties, casually dressed in chinos and a pale blue striped shirt, sunglasses perched on his head, a sweater thrown nonchalantly around his shoulders and knotted in front in a casual style Guy had never quite mastered and, if truth be told, slightly envied.

The shoes were sensible, for walking - Mephistos at a guess - and a leather man-bag and a Sony RX1 were slung over one shoulder. "Tourist". Guy mentally categorised. Reasonably serious amateur photographer too - the RX1 suggested a man who cared enough about the end result to use something better than a small-sensored smartphone. European. Probably French...

Guy recalled one of Bowman's later briefing sessions. 'Brexit is that Jenga brick that you pull out successfully, knowing full well that the next one to go will bring the lot down. Britain has pulled that brick and shown our hand. The next will follow within 12 months - 18 at the outside - and then the whole lot will go.

New alliances are already starting to form and old ones take on new meaning and momentum; the Visegrád Group of Hungary, Poland, Slovakia and the Czech Republic for example, and the more recent Canzuk - Canada, Australia, New Zealand and the UK.

Some are just talking shops, but others have real purpose. We'll doubtless see "Balkanisation" too - the Basques and Catalans have been agitating for years in Spain, for instance.

Even though the likes of ETA has renounced violence like the IRA in Ireland, they won't just stand still and watch the way they are treated fall back to the old nationalist ways. Italy has flirted with leaving the Eurozone and according to our best intelligence will most likely split - North and South, at least - and the Flemings and Walloons in Belgium may finally go their separate ways - *if* they can be arsed...

France is the odd one out, as usual. They do have separatist movements within their borders, of course - Basques, Normands, Corsicans, et cetera - but they are generally pretty ruthless in their suppression of dissent. In public they will cling to Germany like a weeping widow, keeping the fiction of a strong Franco-German alliance alive for as long as possible, but as always they will, like a stage magician, distract attention by saying one thing while doing another.

The new president is not what they appear, by any means. Oh yes, the French are ones to watch; they will stop at nothing to further their national interests - a bit like us, really – which is what puts us once again on opposite sides.'

Guy smiled politely at the new arrival. 'Just a little' he said. 'What gave it away?'

'Your beautiful bag – an English Billingham, n'est pas?

And of course that map you have, which is clearly titled in English...' He waved a hand toward the well-thumbed city map on the table in front of Guy. He had been annotating it with photo-features as he went along - he still had every intention of running another course here soon.

'I will be truthful. It is your map in which I am most interested. I hope you do not mind. I am lost - I am searching for the Santa Justa elevator?' He stuck out a hand with a broad grin. 'My name is Leon, Leon Camus. I am 'ere for business but I must also take some time for myself to see the beautiful city.'

Guy took the proffered hand and shook it. To his mild irritation Camus took that as an indication that he had just made a new Best Friend and pulled up a chair, waving to a passing waiter to indicate that he too would like a small beer.

'Guy Miller. I don't need a map to guide you there. You are quite close already. It's about half a kilometre in that direction.' He pointed to the left. 'Just off the main pedestrianised area. You can buy a ticket at the bottom. It's worth hanging about a bit until dusk, too - it looks good lit up.'

Camus' Sagres arrived and he took a long swig. 'You are most kind, thank you. I am Belgian - from Tournai. There we have nothing similar and...' He leaned forward conspiratorially '...I am a civil engineer by profession. I love such clever constructions and capture them with my own camera.' He put the RX1 on the table with a flourish of pride.

'Nice.' Guy hoped that being monosyllabic might shorten the conversation but Leon was having none of it.

'In your bag... You 'ave a camera too? I always like to know what people use. Canon, maybe, or Olympus?'

Guy sighed inwardly. A different tack was needed. 'Fuji.' He said and pulled out the X-Pro2. Perhaps he *was* being a little churlish, he thought. Perhaps the bloke was genuinely interested.

Leon made an appreciative clucking noise as he bent over to study the camera on the table, then fixed Guy with a beady eye. 'You are Guy Miller... THE Guy Miller? You write the funny guidebooks, n'est pas? I am your greatest fan, *mon ami*! Here, see...'

He produced from his man-bag a dog-eared copy of Guy's second book, the one with a chapter on Lisbon. Camus rummaged some more and pulled out a worn ballpoint.

'Please, do sign. My dear wife will not believe. She thinks I am a fool to laugh at your writing.'

Guy wasn't sure at that point whether he was insulted or flattered, but squiggled his name inside the front cover nonetheless and handed the book back. Camus studied his signature enthusiastically like a man checking a potentially winning lottery ticket.

Guy slipped his own camera back into the Billingham, beckoned to the waiter then reached for his wallet with one hand, picking up the small shot glass containing their drinks tabs with the other. 'Please excuse me, Mr. Camus. I have plans for this evening.' He lied.

'But of course, Guy. You are a busy and important man. Much in demand, *mais non*? But you must *not* pay! It is my pleasure.' He deftly fished a ten Euro note from his shirt pocket. The waiter speared it from his outstretched hand without breaking step and disappeared back inside. Guy expressed his gratitude and stood. Camus scrambled awkwardly to his feet and grabbed his hand, pumping it with gusto.

'*Je vous en prie!* A pleasure, a great pleasure! Enjoy the rest of your time in this lovely city. Take many pictures. I shall finish my beer now and then go to the elevator.

I hope we see each other again!'

Guy concurred politely, shouldered his bag and turned in the direction of his hotel.

Camus sat back down and studied once again Guy's signature in the well-thumbed book. He sat back with a satisfied sigh and sipped at the Sagres, then raised the glass to Guy's retreating back. No, he thought, this would be no challenge at all.

Chapter 6

The next morning was bright and clear. Guy was well rested having retired early after a hot bath to soothe his knee. Irritatingly he found he had developed a small blister on his left big toe as a result of yesterday's walking. A small Compeed plaster now covered it and should, he thought, provide more than adequate cushioning. Now he ran through his plans for the day ahead over a slightly disconcerting breakfast.

Guy had long felt that the hotels of continental Europe had by and large never quite mastered the regional subtleties of the English Breakfast. It surely wasn't that hard, he thought, to fry or poach an egg, cure and grill some decent bacon and put the two together with a mushroom or two and a tomato? Guy regarded his half-eaten plate of fatty smoked ham, bullet-like mini hotdogs and bone-dry scrambled eggs one last time and pushed it away. He'd make do with coffee and *natas* - at least they did those well.

He had already checked out and his backpack sat on the chair opposite. He was expected at the Castelo de São Jorge at 09:00, just as it opened. He would walk in as a tourist, and simply paying the entry fee with his credit card would, he had been assured, alert his intended contact to his arrival. He would then be approached, "validated" and the dispatch handed to him.

After that, it was up to him how he got it and himself to Seville by the following morning. He had elected to take a scheduled Air Portugal flight which departed at 17:45; he had already checked in online and his boarding pass was on his phone.

Plenty of time therefore, he thought, to do a bit more sightseeing before heading off. More of Bowman's words echoed in his head. 'Normal, normal, normal. The Queen's Wayfarers sail through life without drama by simply doing what we do. We don't attract undue attention by deviation from our usual patterns of behaviour, whatever they may be.' Guy understood and appreciated this - in fact something similar formed part of his own course content on street photography.

'You will attract more attention by how you dress and behave than by pointing a camera.' He told his students. 'If you look like you should be there, and that you have the absolute authority to be doing what you do, people will largely treat you as part of the landscape. Act furtive, make jerky movements, look like you are afraid of being caught and you will stick out like a sore thumb.' He finished his coffee, gathered up his pack and headed for the Castelo de São Jorge.

The irony of the chosen location for the rendezvous was not lost on him, he mused, as he walked steadily up the hill to the entrance. It was to have been the original muster point for his now-cancelled course.

Even the time was the same. "Normal, normal, normal", he muttered under his breath as he laboured up the hill the last few yards to the ticket booth.

The queue was short and he stepped into the inner courtyard a few moments later. The morning sun cast deep shadows and he blinked a couple of times before unshipping his pack and fishing out the X-Pro2. There had not been the slightest flicker of acknowledgement or recognition by the cashier and he fleetingly wondered if the technology had worked as Bowman had promised. He slung the camera around his neck, switched it on and half-heartedly framed a bas relief on the cloistered wall opposite.

'Mr. Miller! I am so sorry! I did not mean to be late.' Guy slowly lowered the camera and found standing in front of him a young girl – surely not more than 25 - with an Olympus OM-D slung around her slender neck. She was slender all over, in fact - she looked as if a high wind would snap her in two. A pair of light green eyes peered out under a heavy fringe that was probably fashionable but in Guy's opinion needed a trim. Tight red jeans, a beige Levis jacket and a pair of Converse hi-tops completed the trim picture.

'Late?' He asked, with a sinking feeling in the pit of his stomach 'Late as in…?'

'I am here for your course, of course." She wrinkled her nose and confirmed his worst suspicions. She looked around her then back at him.

'Where is everyone else? Have you set them an assignment already?'

He sighed. An added complication he really did not need. 'Young lady...' He began.

'Almu. Almu Oyarzabal.'

'Almu... I think there's been a bit of a mix-up. I'm afraid the course was cancelled a couple of weeks ago. You should have been notified.' Guy cursed inwardly. He should never have left it to Bowman's people to cancel the course. If you want a job done well, and all that. This girl must have slipped through the net. He didn't remember the name from the last list he printed out, but that wasn't unusual - he generally had a poor memory for names.

Her face fell. He thought for a moment she was going to cry. 'I have come all the way from San Sebastian...' She quavered. 'It is a long way.'

Guy felt like a bastard, even though, technically, it was a cock-up not of his doing. He pulled out a hanky and offered it to Almu then nodded toward the small kiosk in the corner that was already doing a brisk trade in coffee and cake for the early tourists. 'Look, let's have a coffee. You can take some time to relax and give some thought to getting back home earlier than you thought to San Merino.'

'*Sebastian*.' She said with just a hint of irritation. 'San *Sebastian*.' She started to walk in the direction of the kiosk. 'You can at least buy me the coffee.' She said back over her shoulder. Guy sighed resignedly, and followed.

At the kiosk he ordered two coffees and two *natas*. The stout, hair-netted lady behind the counter put everything on a tray.

'Fifteen Euros. May I see your watch?' Guy distractedly peeled off a couple of ten Euro notes and offered them in payment.

'May. I. See. Your. Watch?' The woman said again, emphasising each word. Guy snapped back into focus, thinking furiously.

He proffered his wrist. 'It was a gift from my wife. She has excellent taste.'

'In watches, yes. In men, I think not so much… Here is your change. Put it somewhere safe.'

Guy struggled manfully to ignore the ad libbed insult that the woman had added, clearly as a dig for his not immediately recognising her use of the agreed code phrase. He took the proffered five Euro note and felt taped to the underside the unmistakable shape of a little fingernail-sized micro SD card. He pocketed the note and the dispatch and carried the tray back to the table.

'Excuse me for just a second.' He said, pointing towards the unmistakable sign just a few feet away for the gents toilet. Almu nodded absently and busied herself unloading the contents of the tray onto the table.

Guy ducked into the toilet, found a halfway habitable cubicle and shut himself inside. The dim light flickered on overhead and barely provided enough light to see by. He was surprised to realise that his heart was pounding hard. He took a deep breath - and instantly regretted it. He was not in the most fragrant place in Lisbon, he realised belatedly. He busied himself opening the flap on the side of the X-Pro2 around his neck and ejected one of the two full-sized SD cards inside.

He turned it over in his hand. It wasn't an SD card per se, but actually an adaptor, allowing the smaller cards to be read and written to by a device – such as a camera – which was built to take the larger version. With a fingernail he carefully extracted from the end of the adaptor card a micro SD card identical to the one taped to the banknote.

Working quickly he peeled back the tape and swapped the two cards, putting the precious dispatch into the adaptor and then back into slot #2 in his camera. His own card he placed under the tape on the note and smoothed it back down again before placing it carefully into his wallet.

A quick flush, hand wash, - no towel, or working dryer, of course… and he stepped back out into the sunshine, wiping his damp hands on his trousers.

And stopped.

Almu had company.

Chapter 7

His new "Best Friend" from the previous day sat close beside Almu on a chair he had drawn up from a nearby table for the purpose. As he saw Guy approach, Camus tilted his head to one side and said something conspiratorially to the girl. Whatever it was did not lighten her mood; she looked as upset as before - but also now frightened. Her wide eyes met his and she blinked rapidly as if fighting away more tears. Guy felt a sinking feeling in the pit of his stomach as he noticed that Camus' right arm and hand were out of sight beneath the table and a little too close to Almu for comfort.

'Mr. Camus? I didn't think that I would see my greatest Belgian fan again so soon.'

'Whereas, Guy, I fully expected to see *you* here. Please, take a seat.' He gently shoved the empty chair nearest to Guy with the toe of his boot. Guy took stock of the situation as he eased his pack from his shoulder, placed the X-Pro2 around his neck gently on the table and sat down. The affable Belgian engineer of yesterday was gone. In his place was a harder mien. He was dressed simply today in a nondescript pair of jeans and a crewneck sweater. A pack of his own sat on the floor beside him. Tactical, Guy noted absently, noting the well-worn molle fittings. No Sony or stylish man-bag today.

'Please, Guy, I would ask you to sit on your hands for now, palms down.

Cross your ankles, and tuck your feet under the chair.

I am aware that old as you are, you have some skills, and I would not want to spill this excellent Portuguese coffee all over your young friend.' The tone now was clinical. Much of the accent from yesterday had faded. Guy complied warily. Leon was a very different prospect to a young mugger. He needed to bide his time...

'She is not my "friend". We have only just met. She isn't even supposed to be here. There's been a mix-up.'

'Indeed. I can believe that. But here she is, and that is all to the good.'

'What is going on, Camus - if that is your name?'

'Oh, dear Guy, it is. Allow me to introduce myself more fully. There is no need for subterfuge now. My name really is Camus - Leon Camus. Agent Directeur of the DGER' He nodded his head as he finished as if punctuating his title. 'I would normally add that I am *à votre service*, but in this case, Guy, you are very much at mine.'

'Never heard of it - what is it, a travel agency?'

Camus smiled thinly. 'Not quite. It is the *Direction Générale des Études et Recherches*.

We have but one objective; to ensure the continued existence of the *République Française*.'

Guy snorted. 'Not a Belgian, then. Instead, a French "existentialist" named Camus… how appropriate. Sounds like you're not proper French military intelligence either - that's the DG*SE* isn't it? Blew up the Rainbow Warrior and all that. I've not come across your mob before - it sounds vaguely educational?'

Camus laughed drily. 'You could say that "education" is one of our responsibilities, yes. Education of the other countries of the world that the French nation is not to be ignored or trifled with. For example, you, Guy, are a trifle to be neutralised. We know just why you are here and of your recent recruitment into the ranks of the Queen's Wayfarers. Your seedy little organisation has been a thorn in our side for centuries. Now, they recruit well travelled old men and women once again to ferry their dirty little secrets around, *n'est pas*?'

Guy shifted his weight on the chair. His left hand had already gone numb and his right was not far behind. Camus stiffened and Almu let out a small gasp.

'Keep really still, *mon ami*, until I say otherwise. The young lady has my very sharp Laguiole blade resting just below her ribcage. It would be a great shame to spill Spanish blood because of another little disagreement between England and France, would it not?'

'Basque.' Hissed Almu, speaking for the first time. 'I am *Euskadi*.' Guy noted the fury in her eyes. She appeared at least to have regained much of her earlier composure.

'Whatever. I care not for the Spanish in general. They should have finished the job and crushed your grandfathers when they had the chance under *Generalissimo* Franco. We do not tolerate such as your Basque homeland nonsense in France.' Guy could see that Almu was seething now. He tried to stare her down, willing her not to do anything stupid.

'Now, Guy I have little time for this chit chat. It is time for business. You have on you a small data card, I think. I need you to give it to me now. By doing so you will ensure that, Mademoiselle Oyarzabal will not be harmed. You will do that for me, won't you, Guy?'

'We've just met. I have no responsibility for her.' Guy stared hard at Leon. Out of the corner of his eye he could see Almu's mouth form a small 'o' of astonishment. 'Besides, I have no idea…'

Leon's left hand slapped down hard on the tabletop, making the crockery perform a quick dance. Both Guy and the girl jumped involuntarily. 'Please, Guy, do not take me for a stupid man. You are English. You are a nation of soft fools who put up signs for toads crossing the road. But you have – ethics. You will not sit idly by whilst I hurt the girl. It is not in your nature. The card, please. Now.'

Guy knew in his heart Camus was right.

Regardless, he would not see an innocent woman injured on his account. He looked at Almu for a moment. She stared back, still and silent. Suddenly she jerked. Leon had prodded her with his blade - hard.

'I would remind you that time is not on your side, Guy. Please do not make me get my knife bloody. I use it to cut my fruit.'

'Okay. It's in my trouser pocket. I need to…'

'Move very slowly. Only one hand. Take it out and put it on the table.'

Guy pulled his left hand out from under his leg. A spasm of cramp made him wince. Fingers numb and embossed with the pattern of the chair seat he clumsily extracted his wallet, put it between his teeth and peeled off the topmost five Euro note. He put it on the table in front of Leon.

The Frenchman turned the note over with interest and immediately saw the micro SD taped to the back. He deftly folded it and slipped it into his jeans pocket.

'There. So painless. Now, Guy, this is what will happen now. You will stay here while Mademoiselle Orlazabal and I leave. She will be my... insurance - yes, insurance - that you do not try to be stupid, and follow.

I will leave her at the Elevador de Santa Justa. You have proved you know where it is. In thirty minutes you can find her there - if you so wish. I am a man of my word, Guy. You can trust me for this. Frankly, however, I care not if you come for her or not. I am finished with you, Guy. And you are finished with your mission. Fly to Seville, tell them you are empty-handed. I pity you for what they will say.'

Leon stood and pulled Almu to her feet at his side. Guy caught a glimpse of the thin blade at her side and fought the urge to lunge at the smug French operative. He tried to look Almu in the eye.

'I will come. I will find you.' He tried to sound reassuring but internally his mind was in turmoil. Out-thought and out-manoeuvred by a French bastard who seemed to know his every move - including the ones he hadn't even made yet. Stymied, he watched Leon and Almu walk out of the main entrance, his arm around her like any other romantic couple - if you ignored the unnatural stiffness in her walk.

Guy rose to his feet and almost fell over as circulation returned to his cramped limbs. He steadied himself on the table and snatched up his camera. He flipped the on switch and pointed it quickly at the couple as they turned to the exit in the distance. He had a vague idea of getting a shot or two of Camus to send back to Bowman - perhaps it would help if he could clearly identify him. He nearly dropped the camera in shock as words formed clearly in the electronic viewfinder at his eye:

MILLER

WHAT'S GOING ON

QUERY

Chapter 8

THIS IS BOWMAN
TALK
I CAN HEAR YOU

'Bowman?? What the actual flying *fuck* are you doing in my damn viewfinder??'

WE UPGRADED
YOUR FIRMWARE
WORKS IN WIFI
HOTSPOT RANGE

'Ohh great. So now I have a Ghost in the Machine.' Guy took the camera away from his eye and shook it in sheer frustration. 'Get out!' He paused - and put the camera back to his eye. 'Hang on. *How* are you hearing me?'

USING ONBOARD MIC
NO NEED TO SHOUT

NOW PAY ATTENTION
OUR CONTACT SAYS
YOU HAD UNWELCOME
COMPANY QUERY

Guy looked over at the kiosk. The hairnetted matron stood behind the counter glowering at him. When she noticed his glance she waved a mobile 'phone at him.

'Great. I thought I was on my own. And no toys, you said. Instead you violate my own bloody kit without telling me.'

**STOP MOANING
WHAT HAPPENED QUERY
IS DISPATCH SAFE QUERY**

Guy sighed and glanced at his watch. It would take him about 20 minutes on foot to get from the Castelo de São Jorge to the Santa Justa Elevator. Time enough to update Bowman before he set off. He sat back down and marshalled his thoughts.

'I was intercepted by a French agent. Called himself Leon Camus. Said he was Agent Directeur of the DGER?'

There was a long pause.

**CAMUS AND DGER
KNOWN DANGEROUS
DID HE TAKE DISPATCH
QUERY**

'No. I have it safe.' About an inch from my nose at the moment, Guy silently added. 'But he took a hostage to stop me following him. Young Spanish girl, turned up for the course - which YOU said you had let everyone know was cancelled.'

OOPS
UNFORTUNATE
PROCEED AS PLANNED

Guy let out a long breath. 'Bowman - assuming it IS you and not one of your bloody minions - listen VERY carefully. One. Before I do anything else I'm going to make sure the girl is safe. I'm not letting an innocent party get harmed - not on my watch. Two. Camus knew all about me - and the Queen's Wayfarers. He knew where to find me, and when. You have a mole, Bowman. A big fat one.

The very last thing I am going to do right now is "Proceed as planned." You and yours know my plans, and so it seems does Camus. I'm going off-grid. I'll do your job, never fear - after I have checked on the girl.

Long pause.

NOT HAPPY

'Not bothered. Now I do this my way. I'm not "keeping you posted" either, Bowman, so don't ask. I suggest you do some housekeeping to while away the time. Now, if you will excuse me I have things to do.'

Guy didn't wait for a response, switching the camera off and stuffing it into the depths of his pack. He glanced at his watch and started to walk down the hill in the direction of the Elevador de Santa Justa.

--o-0-o--

A black Renault Twizy whirred softly as Camus piloted it through the still quiet streets. In the seat behind sat Almu. She had very nearly laughed when Camus had led her to the tiny, frog-eyed electric car just outside the gate of the castle but she fingered the narrow slit in the side of her jacket from where he had prodded her with his blade, and thought better of it.

Camus had deftly secured her wrists behind her with a cable tie and seated her in the back, dumping her shoulder bag on her lap. The way that he had negotiated a couple of the corners on the way down the hill had led to her gripping the bag for grim life with her knees as she tried to stop both it - and her - being thrown out of the little car.

Camus halted briefly near to the base of the Elevator and eased his bulk from the driver's seat. She caught his eye and he shrugged almost apologetically.

'It is good for traffic. And it is good for the planet.'

Momentarily taken aback at the Frenchman's unexpected eco-friendliness Almu started to say something but Camus continued in a soft voice.

'...and I cannot ride a motorbike.'

He reached behind her back and cut the cable tie that bound her hands with a single stroke then shoved her bag into her hands and took her by the arm to help her out. It wasn't, Almu mused, the most easy vehicle to climb in and out of and she was glad of her agility.

Camus led her the ten metres or so to the ironwork railings on one side of the flight of steps leading up to the Elevator entrance, slung her bag over her right shoulder and pushed her with her back against the hard metal. From a distance it would have looked like a lovers' embrace - perhaps a little over-enthusiastic, but nothing so aggressive as to raise a concern in a detached observer. Almu writhed in discomfort as she felt his breath on her neck then as he straightened and pulled away she realised that he had fastened her right wrist to the railing with another cable tie.

'Now it is your turn to remain. I am confident Lieutenant Miller will come for you and I would hate for you not to be here.' He grasped her by the shoulders and kissed her briefly on both cheeks.

'*Adieu, petit oiseau.*' He said in a surprisingly gentle tone before turning on his heel and making his way back to the nearby Twizy.

Almu watched him pull away and stood for a further minute or so to ensure he had really gone before reaching into her bag and fishing out a small set of nail clippers. A moment of snipping and she was free. She smoothed down her wrinkled clothes and hair, donned a pair of Persol sunglasses and sat down on the steps to wait for Guy Miller.

--o-0-o--

Leon Camus headed out of the city along the Avenue da Libertade intent on putting some distance between him and Miller. He had taken note of the Englishman's expression when he left him at the castle and had already decided that he did not want to run into him again anytime soon. He was in a good mood, humming softly under his breath. After about ten minutes of driving he left the main road and parked the Twizy in a quiet residential avenue. He fished in his pack and pulled out an Alcatel Go Play smartphone. He cursed as he prised the rubber case off the unit to access the Micro SD card slot and, breathing heavily, un-taped the card from the five Euro note and slid it in.

He fired up the device and used the File Manager facility to access the card. There were only two files on there and they seemed quite small. Their filenames gave nothing away - "One" and "Two".

He clicked on "One" and waited for a moment as the file loaded.

It was a single page. Actually it was a single photograph. Of Miller. Smiling. In what looked like a pleasant English garden - probably his own. He was standing holding an A3 sheet of paper. There were words on the paper, written with a big felt tip pen. It was too small for Camus to read and he pinch-zoomed to make it clearer.

This is not the file you seek

A cold shiver ran down Camus' spine as he read the words. Hands trembling in rage he closed the file and opened the second one. Another photo. Almost identical to the first. Miller's image was grinning now. And the words were different. Pinch. Zoom.

Nope, not here either

Camus smashed his hand into the steering wheel in anger and frustration. The Englishman had made a fool of him. He must have switched the card at some point - probably when he went into the toilets. Camus had foolishly thought it was simply a sign of a weak bladder.

Face set in a mask of fury he threw the phone back into his pack and goosed the Twizy into life again.

Portuguese drivers slammed on their horns and waved their fists as the tiny electric car zipped out of the side road across in front of them and headed back towards the Santa Justa lift.

--o-0-o--

Almu didn't have to wait long. Miller came into view about twenty minutes later, slightly out of breath from the exertion. He was moving in a straight line through the increasing crowds, not even trying to conceal his approach. Almu saw the moment he spotted her as he stiffened and broke step slightly before continuing on at a faster pace. She rose to greet him.

'Are you alright? Did he hurt you?'

'I am fine, Mr. Miller. He did not hurt me. *Putaseme*!' She spat.

'Pardon?'

Almu blushed slightly. 'I am sorry. I did not mean to offend you.'

Guy looked slightly confused. 'You didn't. I was just curious as to what you meant.'

Almu opened her mouth to respond then thought better of it.

'It is a term my mother would not approve of. It describes that filthy Frenchman very well.'

Guy smiled. 'I rather thought it might.' He shifted his weight uncomfortably and glanced over his shoulder. 'Well, as long as you are okay…'

'What will you do now? This has nothing to do with a photography course does it? What is going on?'

'I can't tell you that. I have to go.'

'I have learned from what he said to you that you are something called a Queen's Wayfarer, you had a memory card that you were taking from Lisbon to Seville and that it was taken from you by the Frenchman, who in turn works for a French secret department.'

Guy stared hard at Almu. 'You listen well.'

'And I have a very good memory.' Almu shrugged disingenuously. 'You are going to Spain next, I think. Which is where I need to go myself. She smiled slowly. Are you going to the police? You were robbed, I think?'

Guy paused to think before speaking. 'No. It was a simple mugging, no more. He only got away with five Euros…'

'I am not stupid. There was more to it than that.' Her smile turned into an impish grin. 'Shall I go to the police for you? I could tell them everything and...'

'No. That won't be necessary.'

'I *really* think I should. After all a crime was committed. And to me too - I was threatened and - ab... abducted. And there is a hole in my jacket.' She finished with a flourish, waggling a finger through the offending cut.

'What do you want? Do you want money? I can give you a refund for the course here and now.' He slipped the backpack from his shoulder and unzipped a compartment at the top, pulling out a wad of 50 Euro notes.

'No, Mr. Miller, I just want to go home. You are going to Seville, yes? I have relatives there. I can stay with them for a couple of days then take a train to San Sebastian. Take me with you. I can help.' She paused, thinking furiously. 'I can translate for you.'

'Translate? This is the 21st Century. I have Google. Besides, everyone speaks English anyway.'

Almu started to respond but at that moment there was a commotion at the end of the street. A Renault Twizy flew around the corner and headed rapidly in their direction. Camus could clearly be seen crouched behind the wheel.

Guy looked at the lift entrance. It was about to depart on it's next upward journey. 'Did you get a Lisboa Card?' He shouted at Almu.

'Of course I did - it was in your course joining instructions!'

Guy grabbed Almu by the elbow and propelled her towards the Elevator. They shoved past a couple of tourists by the ticket office, waving their cards and dived through the lift gates as they rattled across. A moment later Camus slammed into the now closed outer door with a furious expression on his face. It was the last they saw of him as they ascended to the upper streets of Lisbon.

Chapter 9

Bowman strode into the dimly lit Ops. Room and slammed the iPad down on the table. Those around him jumped at the loud noise in the usually quiet surroundings. Bowman was noted for two things - his grasp of the myriad operational details of the Queen's Wayfarers day to day activities and his generally calm and phlegmatic manner. He was known as a "low reactor" which gave his current outburst all the more impact.

'This is SHIT.' He said in frustration. 'Whose damn stupid idea was it?'

Nobody answered but a young man stepped gingerly forward.

'Can I help, Sir?' He began 'Sometimes the iPad interface takes a little getting used to by...' He paused. He had nearly said "Older people" but checked himself in time. '...those more used to Android devices.'

'It's not the device, it's the stupid *concept*. We can only talk to Miller when *he* chooses to use his camera, and THEN only when he is in range of a hotspot... with only eighty characters - AND there is no bloody punctuation! I might as well be sending a telegram!'

'It was only intended for dire emergencies, Roger - not idle chit chat. You wanted something discreet and appropriate, remember?'

Bowman turned to face the new speaker. Andre Lucas had been Director of Safety for the Queen's Wayfarers for the past three years and had proven himself adept at the job. "Safety" was a slight euphemism. His directorate had nothing to do with not carrying coffee cups up stairs or running with scissors, but everything to do with getting the Queen's Wayfarers home in one piece if something went wrong.

It was Lucas' team who formed the rapid reaction group which interceded if the keyword was used. If called upon they would do whatever it took to find the Wayfarer and repatriate them - and their dispatch - dead or alive.

'Andre. Glad to see you here. It seems that our new boy Miller has run into a spot of bother first time out. I wasn't chit-chatting, I was trying to find out what was going on.'

Lucas examined his fingernails for a moment. 'I was impressed by Miller when we met. He's not the type to cry wolf. What's happened?'

'Leon Camus is what happened. That French turd put in an appearance and tried to intercept the dispatch as soon as it was passed to Miller.

He says he still has it and is proceeding with the journey, once he has seen to the welfare of a bystander. That's all I know.'

Lucas frowned. 'Camus? He's a busted flush. The old *Direction Générale des Études et Recherches* is not popular with the incumbent in the Élysée Palace these days. They are woefully underfunded and under-resourced in the current climate. Our friends up the river tell me that Élysée would rather fund a *Super Etendard* or two than another five years of DGER field operations. If Camus himself is in the field now it shows just how thin on the ground they really are.'

'Thin or thick, he's turned up, and he's kinetic.' Bowman moved closer and took Lucas by the shoulder. 'Andre, he apparently knew *exactly* where to find Miller, and when. Miller said he knew all about him and his journey. He's gone dark as a result. He doesn't trust us right now - and I can't say I blame him. If Camus had succeeded he could have gone back to Paris in triumph and proved both his own worth and that of the DGER. I don't have to tell you we don't need that right now.'

Lucas looked deadly serious. 'A mole? We have *never* leaked, Roger. All the way back to 1576. Four hundred and forty years of absolute discretion.' He looked over Bowman's shoulder at the other people manning desks and consoles in the Ops. Room, keeping their heads down and trying to look busy

'...and it's a piss-poor time to start now. I'll do some investigating - personally. Do you want me to intercede on the present dispatch journey?'

Bowman thought for a moment. 'No. Discretion is still our best asset at the moment, I think. Miller sounded pissed but in control of the situation. Let him carry on. There are all sorts of unpleasant ramifications if this little matter raises itself onto the radar in Brussels right in the middle of the Brexit negotiations. Stay home for now. But you and your team should be ready to move at a moment's notice.'

'No change there then.' Lucas said with a wolfish grin.

Chapter 10

Guy breathed heavily and massaged his knee as the lift ascended. Clearly Camus had stopped to check the dispatch and discovered that he had fallen foul of one of the "precautionary measures" that Guy had put in place before he left London. It had been a bit of fun that Sunday afternoon in the garden with Jane. She had wondered why he had asked her to take the photos of him with the signs and he had explained. Her quirky sense of humour approved, as he knew it would but then her face had turned serious.

'Hope you don't have to use them in anger.'

'So do I.'

"Anger" was a good word, mused Guy as he straightened and looked at Almu. Camus had been pissed. Severely pissed. She, on the other hand, seemed surprisingly composed for one so young.

"What now?' She hissed, her eyes wide below her fringe. 'We are safe, right?'

'Wrong' said Guy tersely. 'There are stairs…'

Camus was well aware of the stairs, from his reconnaissance the previous day - but his path was not clear. A lot of people chose to ride the Elevator up but stroll down and to his dismay a large tour party from a cruise ship was doing just that.

As he started up he met a wall of brightly coloured man-made fabric, sun visors, sensible shoes, name badges and walkie talkies on lanyards. Directly in front of him was the tour guide herself, half-furled umbrella held aloft, sunglasses perched on top of her head and a look of "don't you dare…" on her face.

Camus dared. He had no choice.

He pushed past the guide and skittled a couple of the tourists out of his way as he started to climb. A brightly coloured wall of indignant polyester immediately closed in front of him and he struggled to make progress in the crush.

'We have to evade and escape.' Guy said, still trying to catch his breath. 'Camus will take the stairs. When the gates open at the top be ready to move - we won't have time to admire the view.'

The seconds ticked by like hours as the Elevator continued its leisurely ascent. Guy hitched his backpack and cinched the straps a little tighter. His heart was pounding and he knew he was building an adrenaline debt but he had to keep going. Beside him, Almu had slung her bag cross-body and looked ready to sprint for Spain - or wherever Basque Country was. Guy was vague on the details and resolved to ask later - if there was a later.

The Elevator ground to a halt with a pneumatic judder and the gates clattered back.

A long walkway stretched in front of them connecting the Elevator tower to the street beyond.

Guy and Almu sped from the lift cage and bolted past the small queue of people waiting to descend, to a chorus of tuts and waved fists. Guy risked a glance over his shoulder at the top of the stairs - no sign of Camus yet, but the hairs on the back of his neck prickled with anticipation and the thought that he might rise into view at any second.

Almu grabbed him by the hand. 'This way!' He complied and found himself being dragged through the doors of a large branch of Zara. Almu rushed through past a gaggle of browsers and headed to an escalator which led upwards. With no better plan of his own in mind Guy let her take the lead. They found themselves a moment later in menswear. She grabbed a couple of items at random off a rail, stuffed them in Guy's arms and propelled him towards the changing rooms.

'In.' She said brusquely. 'You are so tall you stand out in any crowd but especially in a crowd of *Lisboeta*. Stay in there and I'll keep watch.' She pulled off her jacket and stuffed it in her bag then whirled her hair up under a wooly hat. A pair of large sunglasses completed the "disguise".

Guy entered the changing rooms, selected a curtained cubicle and sat down on the chair inside. She was right, of course.

At six feet in his socks he wasn't exactly freakishly tall but he did tend to stand out in a crowd.

He stared absently at the clothes Almu had "selected" - a skinny hooped t-shirt and a pair of jeans, ripped at the knee and sized for a praying mantis. He smiled ruefully and hung them on the hook provided.

For the first time since Camus had taken the initiative at the Castle, Guy had time to think ahead. He mentally ticked off the realities of the situation. He still had the dispatch, safe for now in his camera. He still had to get it to Seville by 11am the following morning. He had an irate French agent for an organisation he had never heard of hard on his tail. Somehow, he had acquired a "helper" - or a hindrance - Guy was not quite sure which. Mentally he arranged the known facts into assets and liabilities, things he could influence and things he could not.

His original plan was in tatters. Camus had mentioned that he was aware of Guy's flight to Seville. Exactly *how* he knew was a problem for another day - and for Bowman - but it was enough for now that he did. It would be complete folly to turn up at the airport under the circumstances. But he had to make the next rendezvous. He thought furiously, and started to formulate a new plan. He had to travel off-grid and he had the germ of an idea as to how it could be done.

Outside the changing room, Almu browsed the racks and kept an eye on both the escalator and a floor-to ceiling glass window that opened onto the street one level down. She ducked back instinctively as she suddenly glimpsed Camus in the crowds below.

He was furiously looking around and quartering the ground in an effort to spot Guy Miller and, she realised with a shiver, her.

She had taken an instant dislike to Camus, not just because of how he had treated her but what he said. She was Euskadi - Basque - and intensely proud of it. She absently fingered a wisp of hair that had escaped from under her hat, thought of the slit in her jacket once more and resolved, if she ever came face to face with him again, to make him pay.

Down in the street, Camus was coming to the realisation that his search was hopeless. With every second that passed his quarry could be putting distance between them in any one of half a dozen different directions. He stopped suddenly and stood stock still. A man barged into him from behind and cursed him loudly in Portuguese for getting in his way. Camus ignored him completely. He shut out the sounds of the street and focused on slowing his breathing. A sense of calm slowly washed over him. He may have lost Guy Miller for now but he knew exactly when and where he was going to be in Seville. He turned on his heel and headed back to the Elevator.

Guy was already on his feet when Almu called his name. He pulled back the curtain and strode out, the clothes in his hand. He handed them to a supremely indifferent shop assistant on the way out, muttering 'Not my colour'. Almu waited for him by the down escalator.

'Camus has gone.' She said, shaking her hair free. 'He went back to the Elevator. I think he went down in it.' She looked expectantly at Guy. 'What now?'

He grinned, feeling back in control for the first time since the Castle. 'I have a cunning plan…'

Chapter 11

An hour later Guy and Almu walked into a small dry cleaners in Rua Castilho. The proprietor tutted in sympathy at the unfortunate damage to the lady's jacket and promised an invisible repair within 24 hours. They received a small blue serial-numbered ticket in exchange and left.

Shortly thereafter they stood on the Rua Rodrigo da Fonseca just across the street from the Four Seasons Ritz Lisboa Hotel. Guy ran through his plan once again and Almu nodded tensely, listening intently to every word.

Guy needed transport to travel the 450 kilometres from Lisbon to Seville by 11 the following morning. The airport was out of the question and he was loath to risk a train - it would be the next most likely mode of transport that Camus would watch and Guy was keen to stay a step ahead.

Time to be creative. Guy had changed and was now dressed more smartly than before, in a pair of black trousers and a plain white shirt. For her part, Almu had acquired a large suitcase on wheels from a charity shop. Guy had not been able to find anywhere in Lisbon that sold smart black shoes to fit his size 13 feet so had had to satisfy himself with a bit of elbow grease to polish up his black Ecco walking shoes to something approximating a shine.

Guy had picked the Ritz Lisboa for a number of reasons. He had stayed there before, years ago on official business and remembered the reception and lobby area layout. It was plush, spacious and quite anonymous. Secondly, he knew it had valet parking and third, there was a big function on tonight. Large BMWs and Mercedes and other luxury cars were already pulling up every couple of minutes and the two valets were kept busy under the direction of the uniformed doorman, taking the cars and driving them around the block to the secure parking a few hundred metres away.

It was nearly 7pm now and the second part of Guy's plan was about to swing into action. He had Googled the number of every taxi firm he could find in Lisbon and ordered a couple of cabs from each company, asking them to collect a large and important party from the Ritz at seven sharp. The need to be punctual was stressed, underscored with the promise of a generous tip.

Guy checked his watch, nodded curtly to Almu and she headed across the street and into the hotel. He hung back a few seconds more, then followed. By the time he had himself crossed the street and started walking along the sweeping entrance drive the first couple of cabs they had ordered had pulled in. He stole a glance over his shoulder and saw another turning off the main road - and two more. By the time he reached the revolving doors of the entrance the drive was effectively blocked by cabs, their drivers starting to get out to see what the hold-up was.

Guy allowed himself a small smile of satisfaction as he entered the doors, did a single revolution and headed out again. The hotel doorman was already involved in a heated discussion with one of the first cab drivers and others were starting to join in, sensing something had happened that might threaten their promised large tip. One of the parking valets looked uncertainly at the cab jam and shrugged - until this was sorted out no-one else could drive in. He sidled off to one side and lit a cigarette. His colleague was nowhere to be found - no doubt he was on his way to the car park.

Into the rising tide of mayhem walked Almu. She emerged from the hotel lobby and somehow managed to get her case stuck in the revolving doors. Nobody could get in or out, and she cried plaintively for help. The already distracted doorman furiously beckoned the idle parking valet and pointed him towards the customer in distress.

Guy had nearly reached the end of the drive now, and the last of the queuing taxis. The next car in line, barely turned in, was a midnight blue late model S-Class Mercedes.

Guy carefully avoided it – it was high enough in value and new enough to have an up to date tracker fitted – maybe even a remote immobiliser. Pulled up behind the Mercedes was a dark red Range Rover Sport, that looked about four or five years old. Guy put on his best smile and stopped beside the driver's window. It descended with a smooth hum.

'On behalf of the Four Seasons Ritz Lisboa I apologise for keeping you waiting, Sir.' The driver, a man in his 40's with a trophy wife at his side barely looked in his direction. 'Valet service. May I park your car for you?'

Range Rover Man looked mildly irritated - it seemed to be his resting face. Trophy Wife sighed theatrically, glaring in displeasure at the 50 metres or so she was going to actually have to teeter in her elegant Louboutins. With a further grimace the driver unshipped his seatbelt and slid out of the car. On the other side his wife did the same. Guy bobbed his head and made grateful noises as he exchanged the ticket from the dry cleaners with a 50 cent coin that Range Rover Man begrudgingly dropped into his outstretched palm.

Guy slid behind the wheel of the big SUV and adjusted the seat to give himself some legroom before slotting it into reverse and pulling back into a three point turn onto the exit road. Three things caught his eye at that point as the world went into slow motion. First was the retreating backs of Range Rover Man and Trophy Wife as they picked their way gingerly down the drive past the melee of cabs and their drivers. Next was Almu, her case freed, heading rapidly in his direction and last the second parking valet, a few metres away, a quizzical expression on his face as he returned from having parked his previous car.

Guy blipped the throttle and was rewarded by the throaty roar of a V8 as he reversed the Range Rover closer to Almu.

She sprinted the last few metres and opened the rear door to lob the case in before diving into the front seat beside Guy. 'Gogogo!' She cried, adrenaline pumping. 'Okay.' He said and lazily swung the steering wheel in a smooth arc away from the kerb. Their path took them past the parking valet who stared suspiciously at their approach. To Almu's horror Guy wound down the passenger window and pulled up beside him.

'Just remembered we left the gas on at home.' He said cheerily. 'Back in a bit.' He handed over a twenty Euro note. 'This is yours if you keep a big space for us. I hate to get my car scratched.'

The Range Rover pulled away smoothly, in no great rush. The valet looked bemused at the note in his hand then slipped it surreptitiously into his trouser pocket and started toward the next car. He didn't understand the wealthy…

Chapter 12

Guy swung the big Range Rover around a large roundabout onto the R. Joaquim António de Aguiar and headed initially for Cascais, following the signs. He had memorised the first few turns from Google Maps and knew he had to get to the A6 to be going in the right direction. He glanced down at the unfamiliar dashboard layout and mused that Land Rover had come on a long way since the Defenders he had occasionally driven in the Royal Navy. In the gathering gloom it resembled the cockpit of a spaceship. He was just about to grope around for the headlight switch when they came on automatically. One less thing to worry about.

Almu was sitting staring straight ahead, her nervous energy spent. she had done well, Guy thought, for one so young. 'Almu... *Almu*' She started and turned to him. 'Please can you figure out the sat nav on this thing and punch in Seville - Calle Dos Catholicos should do it, if it wants a street. Once you've done that please rummage in that bloody case of yours and pull out the biscuits - I need a sugar boost.'

She busied herself with the sat nav controls and five minutes later they had a route to follow and a calm female voice telling them where to go. It was in Portuguese, unfortunately, but it was comprehensible enough for Guy's purposes. She reclined the seat and slid into the back, emerging the same way a couple of minutes later with the biscuits and a couple of bottles of water which she arranged in the cupholders.

The big wheelie case was now surplus to requirements; it had been useful both as part of their distraction and as a temporary container for Guy's backpack and Almu's shoulder bag and their other purchases but they really didn't need it anymore now and she had emptied it and lobbed it over the back seat into the cavernous boot area.

Guy munched on a biscuit as he drove. He had worked out the cruise control and was starting to relax. It started to rain and before Guy could react the wipers sprang into life, batting away the fat drops. They had four hours of driving ahead of them at legal speeds and Guy had no intention, in spite of the temptation of the power under his right foot, of doing it any faster. They had time in hand and he had no desire to attract unwelcome attention.

Biscuit finished, he concentrated on driving but soon realised that the soporific effect of the warm car, the slowly beating wipers and the mental and physical exertions of the day combined were taking their toll.

'Almu!' He barked, making her jump. Talk to me. I need to stay awake while we cover the miles.' He thought for a moment. 'Tell me about your "Basque Country" - where is it, exactly, for a start?'

Almu finished the last biscuit and brushed the crumbs off. 'That is not such an easy question as you think.' She gathered her thoughts and began.

'My home is in a place called Donostia. You may know it as San Sebastian. There is a little film festival that happens there every year.' She smiled in the darkness at her own joke and continued. 'It is in a part of Euskal Herria we call Hegoalde. The name in Basque - more properly our language is called Euskara - means "The Southern piece".'

'Which means, I assume, there must also be a "Northern piece"?' Guy interrupted.

Almu nodded. 'Yes. That is across the border, in France. We call it Iparralde. It is also part of Euskal Herria.'

'So where does this "Euskal Herria" come in? Is *that* what you mean by Basque Country?'

'Almost. The term does not translate that well. The word "herri" has many meanings, including land, people, settlement, town - even state or nation. Euskal is the language so Euskal Herria is most nearly translated as' She paused for a moment to gather her thoughts 'I think it would be "the nation where the Basque language gets spoken."'

'So was it ever one actual country?'

"Nobody can say for certain. It has not been one as such in recorded history.

My people have suffered persecution and discrimination for years by the Spanish and the French who sought to keep us under their control for their own purposes. We have had to fight for so long for recognition, for our language and for the right to live our way of life.'

Guy began to understand some of Almu's anger at Camus' words back at the Castle. It didn't stop him from inadvertently saying the wrong thing. 'I think the only thing I knew before today was about ETA - the terrorist lot. Sort of Iberian IRA...?'

Almu gasped at his words. 'Have you not been *listening*!? ETA are our best hope for peace and freedom! The name translates best in English to "Basque Country and Freedom". We have been oppressed in our own lands, Guy. You are English, you can know nothing of this.' She faltered slightly, then continued. 'We have fought for our rights in the past with the gun and the bomb, particularly during and after the pig Franco. Our leaders have decided to pursue a peaceful path now but it was not always so.' She shrugged and turned pointedly to stare out of the side window. '*Zakila*!' She muttered under her breath.

'Okay, there's no point in insulting me - assuming you just have - if I don't understand what you just said. What does "Zapata" mean?

Almu smiled in spite of herself. 'It means "cock". Which you are for what you said, Englishman.'

'Okay, I apologise. "One man's terrorist is another man's freedom fighter" and all that. You have a point. My country hasn't been ruled by outsiders since the Normans did their stuff in 1066. Please, carry on.'

Almu stayed turned away for another few seconds, then relented. 'Today we do have a sort of self-rule. We have our own schools, universities. But we are not united, not free. It was worse in the past, of course. My great-grandfather and his two brothers were killed by Franco's thugs I had family in Guernica when the Nazis bombed it in 1937. In France it is worse - our brothers are pushed to the margins, treated as second class citizens. Camus represents all that we hate in the French - they put their precious Republic above all else.'

'I see.' Said Guy. 'Well, I think I see why it matters so much to you now.' Silence from the passenger seat. He decided to change tack. 'You have family waiting for you in Donostia?'

Almu nodded. 'My two brothers, one sister, my father, two uncles and six cousins. And my boyfriend.' She smiled and relaxed at last. 'I miss him.'

'How long have you been going out together?'

'Two years now. His name is Xabier. He comes from a good family and he has a good job.

He works for *Festival Internacional de Cine de Donostia-San Sebastián, Sociedad Anónima* - the people who organise the film festival each year.' She smiled. 'Sometimes he gets me in past the security people. I have seen so many big stars, Guy – you would not believe.'

Guy believed. For a moment, by the dashboard light, the resourceful and tough woman that had befriended him and helped him to get this far on his journey looked like a starstruck little girl as she thought of the famous actors and actresses that she had glimpsed from behind the scenes as they accepted their Golden Shell awards.
'Will you marry? I mean...'

'One day, maybe – yes – no – who knows? That is all a long way in the future. We are young – and besides, he hasn't plucked up the courage to ask my father yet.' She giggled. The little girl again.

'How do you plan to get home from Seville? It's still a fair way, isn't it?'

I will take the train. It is comfortable and quick. Not like your British Rails.'

'They are all separate companies now, but I take your point…'

'And you, Guy? How will you get home yourself?'

Guy was silent for a moment. 'That, Almu, is a cracking question…'

--o-0-o--

Seventy kilometres ahead of the Range Rover a Seat Ibiza took the same route to Seville. Camus had lain in wait at the airport but Miller had not shown; somehow he was not surprised. He had ditched the Twizy; being green was one thing but with a range of less than 100 miles before a recharge it was not practical for the journey to Spain.

To be fair, the Ibiza was not much of an improvement; Camus' back was already aching from the uncomfortable driving position in the small car and he was in a foul mood.. The cutbacks in recent years had dug deep into his budget; in the past he would have had a team on a job like this, with two powerful cars and all the intelligence and surveillance backup that they could possibly want.

Now he had to rent a car out of his own pocket and his only real source of inteligence was a mole under the Palace of Westminster who hated the English even more than he did.

Still, he thought, he was still in the game. And tomorrow he would not underestimate Guy Miller a second time.

Chapter 13

Ex-Lieutenant Colonel Andre Lucas was a methodical man, in spite of outward appearances to the contrary. Anyone who judged him solely on his current appearance, however, would be sorely misled. He had been regular army for most of his adult life - Coldstream Guards - and he still bore the stature of a guardsman, but in every other respect he had "dressed down" in his current role of Head of Safety for the Queen's Wayfarers. His hair was long, he had cultivated a well-groomed salt and pepper goatee and his normal work outfit was a rugby shirt and jeans. He was noted for his collection of such shirts, a result of his passion for Rugby Union and his penchant for following the England team around the world on tours.

Lucas regarded his work with the Queen's Wayfarers as akin to air sea rescue. He and his small, hand-picked team were the option of last resort if a Wayfarer "put up a flare" - used the keyword. He had a team of three ready to deploy at all times at each of the cardinal points - Washington, Pretoria, Tokyo and London. If they needed more support than that… well, under normal circumstances overseas there was no more support than that.

The clandestine nature of the Queen's Wayfarers meant that he and his teams really could not be caught running around other people's sovereign states mob-handed.

They tended instead to operate close to the borders - both metaphorically and literally - most of the time, facilitating rapid international extraction - "extracted with vigour", as Bowman was wont to call it.

The last time his men had gone kinetic was during the US presidential election last year. Nobody had been particularly enamoured of Clinton, but the prospect of a Trump presidency had set alarm bells ringing worldwide. Some very specific contingency plans had been put in place by interested parties – plans that were now in effect following Trump's suspiciously unexpected victory at the polls.

The Washington team had been called upon to extract a Wayfarer who had managed to get himself shot and arrested by an over-enthusiastic cop in Benton Harbour, Michigan whilst trying to get his Dispatch safely across the border to the Dominion of Canada. Lucas smiled at the memory; time had not been on their side so it had been an old-fashioned jailbreak, with SIG Sauers instead of Colt .45s. Nobody was hurt, of course - that would have led to even greater complications - but force had been authorised; every time his men stepped into the field, they did so unfettered.

Now, Lucas sat quietly at his desk, deep beneath the Palace of Westminster. It was late and the lights were low. Even the main illumination in his office had cut out because it had not detected movement for some time.

An old fashioned Anglepoise lamp that he had brought in from home cast a pool of warm amber light on the two sheets of paper in front of him.

The first had printed on it the names of everyone he was aware of who knew the details of Miller's journey.

It was a short list, no more than five names including Bowman and Lucas himself.

The second page bore another list, handwritten this time, by Lucas himself. It was slightly longer - seven names in total. The second list was a highly personal one. Each name on it was someone Lucas had some reason to suspect. Some of those reasons, he would be the first to admit, were flimsy to say the least, bordering on slanderous but Lucas prided himself for having a nose for such things and he trusted his instincts, at least to a point.

Only two names appeared on both lists. His issue right now was that one of those names was Bowman. He reached for the phone on his desk and blinked as the room sensors registered his presence and the main lights came on once more. He punched in a number.

"Ravi, it's Andre. I would be grateful if you could do a small job for me."

--o-0-o--

The phone rang and Bowman started from a fitful and uncomfortable sleep. He realised with a degree of irritation that he had fallen asleep in his armchair in front of the TV. Again. The room was cold, and so was he. His wife had clearly gone to bed some time before and the central heating had switched off.

He vaguely recalled her trying to wake him to come to bed then giving up. He gathered up his phone and glanced at the clock on the wall nearby; nearly midnight. The number was one he didn't recognise. He mashed the answer button and waited in silence - sometimes it was just one of those bloody automated PPI calls.

'Mr. Bowman?'

A woman's voice. Educated. Calm. But with a tone of…?'

'Who is this?'

'Mr. Bowman this is Jane Miller speaking. Where is my husband?'

Bowman was caught momentarily flat-footed. 'Mrs. Miller? How do you have this number? This is most irregular, I…'

Jane Miller was not in the mood to hear it. 'MISTER Bowman, I will ask you again. It is a simple enough question. Where. Is. My. Husband?

I am well aware he is on a trip for you but it is now well over 24 hours since last I heard from him. Wherever he is in the world, Mr. Bowman, whatever he is doing, he takes the time to contact me once every day.'

Bowman thought fast. He had a file on Jane Miller as well as her husband. It was thinner, but no less interesting reading. She was not a woman to be fobbed off.

A perfect match for Miller himself, she was noted in the file for being resourceful - and unpredictable. He should have known when he employed Miller he was getting the whole package. Of course Guy had shared his number with Jane - it was what he would do.

'Mrs. Miller - may I call you Jane?' Silence. Like husband, like wife, Bowman thought ruefully. He ploughed on. '...your husband is en route. It is not uncommon for our Wayfarers to choose to go off-grid during a passage for safety and security reasons. I am confident that Guy can look after himself. If there was a problem I'm sure that we would both be the first to know.' A lie by omission but a plausible one, Bowman hoped. He neglected to mention that Guy had gone dark on the Queen's Wayfarers too, and that a French agent was on his case.

Long silence. 'Why should I believe you, Mr. Bowman? When did *you* last hear from Guy?'

'We checked on him this morning, Mrs. Miller. He was well then, and I am sure he is well now.'

Inwardly Bowman cursed. Guy Miller had broken a cardinal rule. He understood why, but it was now causing him a headache. Normal, normal normal. It was *normal* for Guy to check in with Jane daily. It was routine, and he had broken routine. As a result, Bowman now had a potential problem in Jane Miller.

'Mrs Miller, you have my word that as soon as your husband gets back in contact with us I will let you know, okay? All I ask in return is if he contacts you first you extend to me the same courtesy.'

Long silence. So long that Bowman checked his phone display to see if the signal had dropped. His home had thick walls and reception could sometimes be a little flaky.

'Very well Mr. Bowman. I am well aware Guy is due to be in Seville today. I shall wait a little longer to hear from him - or...' there was an unmistakable chill in her voice '...from you.'

Bowman fervently hoped that Guy would contact his wife soon, if not first. Her next words underlined his view.

'Make no mistake, Mr. Bowman, if anything happens to my husband you will have me to answer to. And you do not want that. Goodnight Mr. Bowman.'

'Goodnight Mrs. Miller.'

Jane Miller put down her mobile, took a deep breath and fussed the large tabby cat sitting on the table in front of her. He had been mute witness to the whole conversation. Now he leaned forward and buffed his forehead against Jane's. She fussed him and he purred, deep and loud. The sound and the unconditional love it represented helped calm her nerves.

'Where's your daddy, eh? Where's he gone?' Be safe, Guy, she fervently thought. He could be a pain in the arse sometimes, but he was *her* pain in the arse. She reached for her wine glass then thought better of it. She poured the last of the wine down the sink in the kitchen, gathered up the cat and went to bed.

Chapter 14

Guy was momentarily disorientated as he was woken by a staccato thrumming noise that reminded him of a Bofors anti-aircraft gun. It took him an instant to remember that he was driving on a Spanish motorway at 120 kph in a stolen Range Rover and to realise that the noise that had woken him was the wide, low profile tyres thumping over the reflective cat's eyes between lanes. He jerked the wheel over and fishtailed the big SUV for a heart-stopping moment before regaining control.

Almu stuck her head between the seats, from the back seat where she had been asleep for the past hour.

'What are you doing Guy? Are you trying to kill us??'

'Trying, no. Almost succeeding, yes.' He rubbed furiously at one eye and wound the driver's window down. A blast of noise and cold air chilled the stuffy cabin of the big Range Rover in an instant.

'I need to pull over. Get some sleep.' He squinted at the dashboard 'And we need fuel. This thing wasn't full to start with and it drinks like the Queen Mother at Ascot. There's time. We've made good progress from Lisbon and we have a few hours in hand.'

Almu looked bemused at the reference to the Queen Mother but understood the sentiment.

She pointed to a sign they were just whizzing past. 'There is a service station just ahead. We can stop there. I need a break anyway, and we can get some food and something to drink.'

Guy glanced down at himself guiltily. Even by the dim glow of the dash lights and the intermittent illumination cast by the overhead street lights he could see that he was covered in biscuit crumbs; he had munched at regular intervals to help him stay awake.

'Coffee.' He muttered. 'And I need to call my wife. We always talk, or at least, text, every day and with all that has been happening in the last few hours I'm running very late. She will be worried.'

Almu nodded. 'She must be a special woman to be with you. You must call her.'

Guy looked sideways at Almu, not sure whether she had insulted him - again - or not. Perhaps she still bore a grudge from their previous conversation...? He eased off the throttle, indicated and swung the wheel smoothly to the right as they slowed and exited the E1 onto the ramp for the services.

Even at this early hour it was well-lit and open, although hardly busy. It was a modern building, but a few years old; the signs and windows looked like they could do with a thorough wash, although the interior itself looked warm and welcoming.

He pulled up at a pump first and filled the tank - it amused him to think that the owner would be reunited with his car with more diesel than before, albeit a few hundred more k's on the clock. He walked stiffly to the small kiosk, paid cash and re-parked the car a short distance from the building, facing out.

They walked inside and blinked at the brightness and the warmth. Guy immediately appreciated that it wasn't like a motorway service station in the UK - no Starbucks, Smiths or Burger King, he noted with approval. Instead there was a small, clean café with formica tables and a counter behind which a gleaming coffee machine gave him hope of a decent brew. Almu was ahead of him to the counter and had started to raid a clear plastic cabinet in which there were filled rolls - "boccadillos" - Guy corrected himself - and an assortment of pastries and tarts.

Suddenly weary and with an urgent need to wee - he had been alright all the time he was sitting in the car - he thrust a handful of notes into Almu's hand and headed to the toilets. Relieved, he washed his hands and caught sight of himself in the mirror.

He looked drawn and red-eyed. Sleep was essential, he thought. A quick refresh, then an hour or so reclined in the car should do it.

He stepped out and headed to a payphone he had noticed on the way in. He was loath to use his mobile in case it was traceable. It was lower-risk, he thought, if he used a public phone.

The call connected quickly and he heard the familiar British ringing tone. He imagined Jane would still be in bed at this ungodly hour and expected it would take her a moment or two to wake up and reach over to the phone extension on his side of the bed. He was surprised therefore that his wife answered after less than three rings.

'Sweetheart it's me. Sorry to ring so late, I…'

'Guy! I have been so worried about you. Are you alright? Where are you?'

'I'm fine. I just had to change my plans just a little. There's a bit of interference on the line, originating from France. It put me behind a bit. I've been making up the time though, and all is well.' He had already decided not to go into detail and to be deliberately vague; it was safe to assume that the phone he was using was not tapped, but Camus had known so much about him that he couldn't rule out an intercept on his own home landline.

'Are you safe, Guy? This isn't like being a Messenger.'

Too true, he thought, but his response was a study in reassuring neutrality. 'I'm completely safe and unharmed, Darling. Just missing you, and being at home. I'll finish up in Spain and be back as planned before you know it.'

Jane Miller was unconvinced, but knew when to keep her own counsel. She sighed and responded in kind. 'Alright you, just keep buggering on, eh? Home in one piece, please. I love you.'

'And I love you. I'll be in touch but please don't worry if I'm quiet for a bit. Not all ears are friendly.'

'I understand.' Jane's voice was a little husky. 'Be a good Guy.'

He smiled at the in-joke. 'Yes Dear.'

--o-0-o--

Jane Miller put the phone back on the charging base and reached for her mobile, fully intending to text Bowman. She even started to type a message, then thought better of it. Bugger him, she thought. He can stew until the morning. She put the mobile back on the bedside table and snuggled down again, on Guy's side of the bed. In all his travels she had never told him that in his absence she slept where he normally lay. His ego was big enough already.

Chapter 15

Half deaf, completely stiff and exhausted, Leon Camus allowed the Seat to coast to a halt at the fuel pumps. He topped off the tank and morosely perused the chocolate bars and fizzy drinks that were the extent of the kiosk's inventory. He had lost valuable time over a hundred kilometres back by taking a wrong exit. It had taken him some time to realise and to thread his way back to the E1.

He was now behind the schedule he had set himself and keen to press on; much as he wanted to rest, he felt he had to keep going, which meant eating this disgusting fare behind the wheel. He stood by the car for a few moments glaring angrily at the no smoking signs that surrounded him. He contemplated pulling over by the main service area and enjoying a single quick cigarette before getting hack on the road. There were only a few cars in the car park at this early hour, a Passat, a couple of Peugeots, a Seat Ibiza similar to his own – another hire car? And an incongruously shiny Range Rover with darkened windows.

A hundred metres away, Almu sat in the passenger seat of that same Range Rover, transfixed by the sight of Camus standing so close. She and Guy had eaten, freshened up and changed into warmer clothes then returned to the car. Guy had reclined the driver's seat and caught about an hour of fitful sleep while Almu had kept watch. They weren't expecting any trouble but Guy was on his mettle now and was leaving nothing to chance.

He had told Almu to wake him after an hour and she had just done so.

Guy had gone back inside to answer one more call of nature before they headed on to Seville. He had been gone a couple of minutes when Almu had first noticed Camus. Now, to her horror, as Camus looked in their direction, Guy strolled out through the automatic doors and headed straight in her direction. Her mind whirled. Perhaps they would be lucky. Perhaps Camus was looking in their direction but but not actually seeing. Perhaps he was short-sighted. Perhaps it wasn't actually him…

Her hopes were shattered as she saw the Frenchman suddenly straighten and drop the small white plastic bag he had emerged from the kiosk with. Guy had not noticed and was still ambling toward the back of the big Land Rover, with about fifteen metres still to cover.

Almu and Camus reacted simultaneously. He fumbled with his keys to unlock his car again as she scrambled across the big centre console and dropped into the driver's seat. "Dropped" was the operative word - the seat was bigger than any armchair she had at home and was currently adjusted to Guy's tall frame. He was nearly a foot taller than her and as it was she could hardly see over the steering wheel let alone reach the pedals. The key was in the ignition already and she mashed the dimly glowing "Engine Start/Stop" button.

For a heart-stopping instant nothing happened. Then she remembered what she had seen Guy do earlier. You had to depress the footbrake to start the engine... She wriggled to the edge of the seat and got a toe on the brake pedal then stabbed at the button once more.

The big V8, still warm, burst into life with a throaty roar. She groped and found the seat reach adjustment and thumbed it forward. An electric motor smoothly, almost politely propelled the seat towards the dashboard, agonisingly slowly. She risked a sidelong glance; Camus was behind the wheel of his own car now and the headlights reached towards her, then jerked as he got it into gear and started to move.

The passenger door burst open and Guy threw himself in.

'Drive!' He barked. 'Floor it! Get us mobile before he T-bones us.'

Camus had his foot hard down as he accelerated towards them. He had no plan beyond ramming the car – where the Hell had Miller got *that* from, he took a moment to wonder - and stopping him before he escaped. The stupid Spanish girl was an irrelevance and Miller himself was proving to be a troublesome annoyance.

He would end this right here, right now. The Range Rover was still stationary as Camus' Ibiza picked up speed.

He had to jink around a couple of high kerbs in his path then slammed the car down a gear and heard the engine protest as he put his foot hard down. He aimed right at the centre of the bigger vehicle and shut his eyes as he braced for the inevitable impact.

The Range Rover Sport, in spite of the name, was not designed for quick getaways. The engine, though large and powerful, was low-revving and leisurely with low-end torque more of a priority than outright speed. The turbo lag didn't exactly help either. Still, Almu buried the accelerator pedal in the thick Wilton carpet and prayed.

For an instant nothing happened... and then everything happened at once. The Range Rover rolled forward slightly then the turbo cut in. Almu and Guy were pushed back in their seats as power was fed smoothly to all four wheels simultaneously and nearly two tonnes of British steel started to move. Then the hire car hit.

Camus had seen the big SUV start to accelerate and had tried at the last minute to correct his trajectory. He succeeded, but not quite enough. He struck the flank of the Range Rover just behind the rear wheel. The impact threw him forward and his forehead smacked against the steering wheel as he spun and came to an abrupt halt.

Almu and Guy were tossed from side to side by the impact. The tail of the Range Rover was thrown to one side and they felt for a heart-stopping moment that they were going to flip over as it balanced on the two right hand wheels.

Normality came back with a bone-jarring crash as the Land Rover's low centre of gravity re-asserted itself and the car smashed back down on all four wheels. The impact had slewed them around and Almu could see clearly that Camus was motionless in his car, held upright by the seatbelt. As she watched, he sat up and turned to stare straight at her.

'Almu! Drive! Get us out of here!' Guy was leaning forward in his seat, looking at Camus and his car. She pushed down hard on the accelerator again and the Range Rover, dented but still largely undamaged, made off like a dirty dog at bathtime.

Camus rubbed his neck ruefully. His forehead ached from the impact with the steering wheel and he wiped a trickle of blood from one nostril. Amazingly his engine was still running. He seemed to still have one headlamp although it's beam was shining off to the left at a crazy angle.

The Range Rover was gone. He caught a glimpse of it in the distance as it pulled out onto the E1 headed East. Grimly he reached under his jacket, pulled out a well-worn 9mm Beretta, racked the slider, put on the safety again and laid it carefully on the passenger seat beside him.

Then he gunned the engine and gave chase.

Chapter 16

Inside the Range Rover Guy took stock. Almu was shaking and he didn't feel too clever himself. He stared hard at her by the dashboard light. She looked ashen, but in control. For his part his knee had taken a hefty bash against the armrest and was throbbing painfully. Nothing was broken but it was certainly not happy. They were back on the motorway now. There were interesting noises coming from the rear suspension and a couple of warnings on the display, but overall they still seemed to be in one piece.

Their issue now, Guy mused, was that they were heading in the right direction but they were on a sparsely populated stretch of road with no exits for the next 19 kilometres. Guy hadn't seen Camus get his car moving before they were out of sight but he was under no illusions - the Frenchman had just upped the ante and the gloves were well and truly off. If he could still pursue he undoubtedly would.

'Ease off the throttle just a little.' He said gently. They were doing in excess of 160kph now and stood out like a sore thumb. Almu complied and tucked in, in front of a big Volvo lorry. Smart move, thought Guy.

'Camus will follow, if his car is still capable. A stern chase is a long chase, but given enough road he can close the gap. No matter what, we need to be out of his sight when we reach the first turn-off.

I don't intend to take it - according to the signs there's another, just three clicks further on that will suit us just as well. In any event he will expect us to take the first - I hope.'

Almu was quiet for a moment. She had never driven anything the size or power of the big Range Rover before but she was rapidly getting used to it. She glanced in the rear view mirrors. The stretch of road they were travelling on wound through a thickly wooded area and she couldn't see the road behind for more than about half a kilometre.

It had started to drizzle again and the few headlights she could see betrayed nothing about the vehicles they were attached to. The drizzle increased and reduced everything to crystal star trails as she watched.

'Earth to Almu…?' Guy prodded.

'I am fine.' She reassured him. 'I can see no trace of him.' She let out a long breath. 'Perhaps…'

Another sign flicked past. 14 kilometres to the next exit.

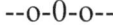

--o-0-o--

Seven kilometres back and closing rapidly Camus was concentrating hard. His one remaining headlight had given up the ghost within minutes and he was now effectively driving half blind. At some point the windscreen wiper on the passenger side had disappeared but the in front of him on the drivers' side was still in the game and struggling gamely with the wet conditions, skipping and shuddering but still giving him a smeary view of the road ahead.

Overall, the little Seat was protesting but holding together; he was actually quite surprised by the punishment it could take and still keep moving. He was regretting his impulsive action now - he should have stayed cool and pretended he has not spotted Miller and tailed them instead from a distance - but he hadn't done that and now he felt he was committed to follow through.

He studied the road ahead. It was still early, not yet dawn although the first hint of light was creeping into the Eastern sky. He wiped the last trickle of blood from his nostril and urged the battered car on harder.

--o-0-o--

Two kilometres to the first exit. Guy allowed himself a sigh of relief. To the truck driver's obvious frustration they had stayed just in front of the big Volvo lorry all the way and the two cars that had passed were clearly not Camus. They might just make it.

'Still keep going?' Asked Almu.

'Nooo...' said Guy slowly, weighing up the options. 'Let's drop off and follow the signs on the smaller road for a bit. We're close enough to Seville now for it to be signposted all the way, judging by the signage. There's no sign of our French friend, so let's not push our luck, eh?' Almu nodded, and eased off the throttle. The Volvo lorry snorted like a wild beast as the driver dropped a couple of gears and pulled out to overtake.

A sharp crack, then another and the passenger door mirror then the rear window of the Range Rover shattered in glittering showers of glass. The roar of the exhaust multiplied in volume and the temperature plummeted. Almu screamed and ducked instinctively and the big SUV danced across the road. Guy grabbed the wheel with his left hand and fought to keep them steady.

No more than ten metres behind was Camus in the Seat. He had spotted them a few minutes ago, on one of the sweeping bends. His dead headlights had kept him inconspicuous just as their own tail-lights - one blown out by his earlier action - had betrayed their identity. He had tucked in behind the same lorry and bided his time, using it as a blind in the same way as they were. Now he was right there, holding the Beretta in his left hand and steering with his right and taking aim for another shot.

Almu had regained her composure and her grip on the wheel. She had her foot hard down again, but traffic was already beginning to thicken even at this early hour and she was dodging other, slower moving traffic in front of the Range Rover as she struggled to get enough elbow room to use the full power of the big V8 to once more put some distance between them. They had missed coming off in the heat of the moment and were stuck again on the main carriageway, at least for two more kilometres.

A shot spanged off what was left of the passenger door mirror and Guy flinched instinctively. Nowhere to run, nowhere to hide, he thought. Nearly at the next exit though...

'Almu, it's time to go on the offensive.' He said curtly.

Ease off a little, let him drift closer, then when I say, slam on the brakes - hard.'

Almu glanced across at the set expression on his face then nodded quickly without a word. Guy turned in his seat and watched intently as Camus closed the gap. He must have been travelling at the very limits of his already damaged car to catch them up. He watched as Camus raised the Beretta once more and took the best aim he could at one of their fat rear tyres.

'Wait... wait... NOW!'

Almu almost stood up from the driver's seat as she pulled herself up on the steering wheel and put both feet and all her weight on the brake pedal. The sophisticated anti-lock brakes and traction control systems of the Range Rover cut in instantly and worked to bring them smoothly and safely to a halt. The tail-end impact of Camus' hire car hit them like a thunderbolt.

Camus had almost no warning; he was too close, the Range Rover's brake lights were both dysfunctional and he had a fraction of a second to realise what was happening. He dropped the Beretta and gripped the wheel, wrenching it hard to the left as he tried to avoid the collision.

He failed. The little Ibiza hit the back of the Range Rover almost full on. It was an unequal fight. With a deafening metallic whump the two cars smashed together for the second time in twenty minutes. This time though, the Seat came off far worse, as did Camus. He was thrown forward like a rag doll, his head smacking the steering wheel again.

This time the airbag deployed, stinging his face with a thousand pins and needles and temporarily rendering him deaf and blinded. Stunned, his feet slipped from the pedals and his car drifted onto the hard shoulder, coming to a halt against the crash barrier.

In the heavier, better built Range Rover Guy and Almu had fared a little better, but not much.

Knowing what to expect they also had time to brace, which had helped – a little. Almu was groggy, but Guy himself had hit his head hard against the B pillar and was not moving. Their car had stalled and the dash was lit up like a one armed bandit. They were still rolling too, but across the carriageway toward the central reservation, straight into the traffic approaching rapidly from behind.

Almu gathered her senses and hit the brakes. Without the power assistance provided by the engine it took all her strength to stop the big car. She found she couldn't steer - it was just too heavy. Beside her Guy moaned and muttered. He was starting to come around. Almu turned her attention back to trying to regain control of the car. She scanned the dashboard and went through the starting procedure once more. The four litre V8 roared into life, far louder than before - clearly their exhaust had been one of the casualties - but even over the booming roar of their own engine Almu jumped at the sound of the air horns on the articulated lorry bearing down on them.

The truck - almost a twin of the one they had unsuccessfully used as a hide - was travelling at speed as the driver saw the crash happen just ahead. It looked from the driver's elevated vantage point like the bigger car in front had slammed on the brakes… Surely not... That would be insane...

No time to think now. One hand hammered down on his hazard flashers and he dropped down the gears as he hit his own brakes.

He flipped on all his spot, fog and running lights turning the front of his massive truck into a council-house just before Christmas. As the Range Rover came to a halt diagonally across his path he knew instinctively that he was going to hit it.

Sound the horn, at least give the poor bastards a fighting chance before...

Almu flung the Land Rover into gear and uttered a childhood prayer as she pushed the accelerator pedal through the floor. They would not survive another impact, especially from that thing. A wall of lights was bearing down on them, illuminating the inside of the car as if it was midday. For a second time the ability of the big SUV to deliver low-down torque when needed came to their aid. With a shudder it started to move then the smooth power of the turbo cut in once more and Almu felt as if a big hand had scooped them up and was shifting them to safety.

In their wake the lorry slid to a halt, itself now blocking two lanes. Almu accelerated hard and headed off at the exit, fighting the twisted chassis that wanted to take them off at an angle. Guy was awake now, though not speaking. They exchanged glances. This was not going to end well.

On the E1 Camus lay prone at the wheel of his shattered hire car. The truck driver regained a measure of control, both self- and vehicle, and pulled over just ahead of where the Seat had come to rest then ran back to help.

Behind him were a couple of minor shunts as other drivers had fought to avoid a big pile-up. What a mess. He put in a call to the emergency services. He wasn't going to make his next delivery on time...

Chapter 17

Guy's head felt like someone had played keepy-uppy with it. Wearing steel toe-cap boots. He had a lump the size of a duck egg coming up on his temple and he felt like he had cracked a tooth. His knee, already wrenched in the earlier excitement, was on fire now. He sat up with a theatrical groan and tried to pay attention to the road ahead.

They were travelling noisily and at some speed along a single-carriageway road. According to the signs they were approaching a town by the name of Palomares del Rio. The battered Range Rover was lurching like a drunken sailor and half the dashboard telltales were shining an angry crimson. An ominous flapping noise came from the nearside rear; if the tyre had not actually blown it was on the way out any minute. The Sun had risen now and a thin watery light painted everything around them in sombre hues.

'How far do you think we are we from Seville now?' Asked Almu, scanning the road signs ahead.

'About 20k, I think, give or take. That's probably about 19k further than this car will take us. We need to lose it and find another means of getting there.'

Almu pointed at an unmistakable symbol on the sign just ahead. 'There's a train station here. There must be trains…'

'Excellent. That will do nicely.' The sign indicated that the station was no more than a kilometre from their current location. Guy pointed at a large patch of waste ground a few hundred metres ahead. The rain had stopped, but it was pockmarked with greasy looking puddles and some clumps of spindly buddleia. A rusty dump truck and a couple of vans were parked there together with an ancient flatbed lorry.

'Let's lose our Landy there. She's a liability now.'

Given the noise from the blown exhaust and the by now definitely flapping rear tyre they had little choice. They were already attracting unwelcome attention from early risers.

They bumped down off the metalled surface of the road and onto the uneven mud and gravel. A loud bang and a sudden lurch announced the final demise of one of their rear tyres. Almu managed to keep control long enough to coax the Range Rover behind the dumpster and switched off the ignition with a sigh of relief. The abused engine ticked and popped as it cooled. Guy let out a long-held breath and looked at her quizzically.

'Do you want to bale out now? This is hardly your fight, and it has got a lot uglier than I ever dreamed when I allowed you to tag along. We're in Spain now. You can get a train home to San Sebastian quite easily from here, I should think.'

Almu shook her head.

'I can get a train easily from *Seville*, not from here, and I have a cousin who lives there that I really ought to visit since I am here. We both still have to go in the same direction for now.' She responded with a small shrug, then beamed. 'You cannot get rid of me that easily, Guy Miller.'

Guy snorted, then nodded. 'Okay, okay. Just giving you the option. I take your point. C'mon, then. We have a train to catch.' With that he prised open the warped passenger door with a creak, stepped out and promptly fell over.

Almu gasped, tried to reach across, thought better of it, darted out of the driver's door and hurried around the front of the car, slipping and sliding in the mud herself. Guy was back on his feet, trying to brush off the mud and looking more than a little annoyed with himself. He brusquely waved her away.

'I'm fine, fine. Don't fuss.' He muttered testily. 'My damn knee gave way, that's all.' He put weight on his leg again and hobbled a couple of paces. 'Ahh...'

'"Ah" indeed.' Said Almu. 'You are *not* going to be sprinting about on that.'

Guy looked despondent. 'It will ease up with use. It's just a minor thing. I had an accident years ago and it still troubles me occasionally.'

He gingerly put his weight on it once more and winced, then wrenched open the Range Rover's rear passenger door and retrieved his backpack from where it had come to rest in the footwell. He fiddled with a couple of straps and freed from the front of the bag a small Velbon monopod, which he proceeded to extend and test to see if it would support his weight.

'"Occasionally" - like having two car crashes within an hour?' She studied him as he fiddled with the monopod, adjusting the length. 'What do you plan to do with that? This is hardly the time for a picture.'

'I carry this bloody thing worldwide. Have done for years. I hardly use it, because I hate to tie my camera down. But now it can earn it's keep, as a walking staff.' He eased on the backpack, then slipped his hand through the wrist strap at the top of the monopod, gripped it firmly and started to walk slowly in the direction of the railway station. Almu looked after him for a moment, shook her head with a wry smile, scooped up her own bag and set off in Guy Miller's wake.

--o-0-o--

Traffic officer José Benito stared again at the small white business card in his hand. It was crumpled, slightly bloodstained but the telephone number thereon was clearly legible. A Paris number, which he had dialled 40 short minutes ago.

His shift had all started out fairly normal. A call to attend a road traffic accident on the E1.

Urgent as always - it was a major artery in that part of Spain and the main part of his daily duties was to help keep it free flowing - but this time the dispatcher had mentioned casualties so he had approached with particular trepidation - he had dealt with more than his fair share of fatalities over the years and it always unnerved him.

This one was at least sitting up. He had what looked like a broken nose and various other bruises and contusions but he had survived what showed all the signs of being a really nasty smash. His car was a write-off, for sure; Jose had already done a vehicle check and established that it had been hired in Lisbon the previous day. The unfortunate driver would be filling in forms for months, he mused.

So far so normal. Then it started to get odd. Of the other vehicle involved there was no sign. The truck driver – himself shaken but a surprisingly good witness - had reported a dark coloured English Land Rover – an older model Range Rover Sport, he thought.

He said it had taken off at speed in spite of some obvious damage to the rear. It wasn't unheard of for innocent people to leave the site of an accident; traumatic shock could sometimes do funny things to otherwise normal people - but there was something strange about this one.

Then it got more odd still.

The driver of the hire car - his driving licence tallied with the hire car information and showed him to be a French national named Leon Camus - had said nothing about what had happened, simply handed him this plain white business card and asked him, very politely but very insistently, to call the number thereon.

He had then sat perfectly still as the paramedics dressed his wounds and checked him over. Normally José would have ignored such a request - this was *his* investigation site and *he* would decide what happened - but there was something in the Frenchman's calm and authoritative manner that gave him pause.

When the number connected a voice answered immediately. It spoke clearly, albeit in French. '*Votre identity*?' it had said.

José identified himself by name, rank and district and the voice switched seamlessly to Spanish. The next question shook him more than anything up to that point. 'Did you take this card from a dead man?' José assured the voice that Camus, although battered, was still alive. '*Bon*. He will be extracted immediately. Please confirm your exact location.' José did so and the line went dead.

A few minutes later, his phone rang. It was a mobile number he did not immediately recognise, but the first five digits were the same as his own. He answered.

'Officer 1479 Benito?'

The new voice was Spanish, a local accent. Brusque and impatient-sounding. José confirmed his identity and badge number.

'This is Chief Commissioner of Police Hernando Cortes. I am told you have a French man with you. You are to keep him safe and give him every assistance. Keep the E1 closed at least until he is ...collected. Do you understand?'

José acknowledged. He knew of Cortes, of course. He sat four - no, five - levels above him in the police service and was responsible for all the law enforcement operations in the Province of Seville.

Cortes ended the call abruptly with the simple instructions - no, *commands* - 'Don't ask any questions. Don't even *talk* to him unless he talks to you. And Benito, do *not* fuck this up.'

That was half an hour ago now. The E1 was still closed, and traffic had built rapidly. Arguments had started to break out between trapped motorists, increasingly fractious at the delay and apparent inactivity.

José left his colleagues to deal with that and stood fingering the card, watching the man Camus out of the corner of his eye. He was was walking about now, with a slight limp. He had a foul-smelling French cigarette between his lips and was pacing back and forth.

Both men heard it at once. A faint whup-whup of rotor blades, approaching rapidly.

José scanned the sky in the direction of the sound then spotted a large, dark coloured helicopter hugging close to the ground not more than a kilometre out. Unusually and, thought José, illegally, it showed no running lights as it approached.

The pilot clearly knew very well where he was going and what he was doing. The big helicopter reared up just short of their location then touched down lightly on the deserted Eastbound carriageway of the E1, throwing a cloud of dust over him, the paramedics, his fellow police officers and Camus.

He glanced over at the Frenchman who had pulled a pair of slightly incongruous aviator-frame sunglasses from a pocket and put them on to protect his eyes from the debris being thrown up by the rotor blades. His battered pack, retrieved from his even more battered car, was slung over one shoulder and he ground the stinky French cigarette he had been sucking on under one boot-heel. He might have looked cool, thought José, had one lens not been cracked.

The side door on the helicopter slid back and José suddenly tensed as two heavily armed soldiers stepped out. His right hand moved instinctively towards his own holstered sidearm but one of the masked and goggled men swung his machine pistol in the police officer's direction and he rapidly decided it was not the day for heroics - or for stupidity.

Instead he watched silently as Camus scuttled, head bowed, to the open side door and was helped aboard. The two soldiers scanned the scene once more and climbed back aboard themselves. A moment later the helicopter lifted into the sky with a roar and turned back in the direction it had come.

Funny thing, thought José, as he watched it fade to a dot in the distance. The helicopter carried only shaded-out insignia on it's fuselage. A couple of barely-legible serial numbers and the unmistakable circular star emblem of the European Union. But he had glimpsed the shoulder patches of the two soldiers. The colours were muted but instantly recognisable. The three broad bars formed the tricolour of France.

Chapter 18

Aboard the helicopter, Camus had been handed a set of noise-cancelling headphones and had been helped to strap in by the loadmaster, who now sat beside him. The two soldiers who had stepped out on the E1 sat opposite, their masks discarded. That made their thoughts no more readable, as they sat silently staring into space. In the cockpit the pilot and co-pilot busied themselves with their instruments.

A voice came over the headset - the pilot. "Monsieur, our instructions were to recover you, give you whatever assistance you need and take you to wherever you want to go. Where is that?'

'Seville' Camus said flatly. ' Close as you can to the centre of town.'

'*D'accord.* Twenty minutes, twenty five at most, dependent on ATC permissions.' The pilot was not exactly chatty, which suited Camus. A moment later he felt a slight shift in their direction and an acceleration.

'Can I make a telephone call on this thing?'

A new voice - the co-pilot?

'*Oui.* We can patch you through. Do you know the number you want?'

Camus knew it off by heart. It was the same number on the card he carried, dialled by the Spanish traffic cop. He recited it slowly and waited. A ringtone in his headphones lasted no more than a second before the call was answered.

'*Votre identity?*'

'Camus, Leon. Agent Directeur. DGER. Authorisation: Henri. Louis. 1427641, Oscar.'

A pause. Camus knew that the authorisation alone was not enough. His voiceprint was also being processed, his identity and authority confirmed beyond any doubt.

<Click>

'*Oui. Monsieur le Directeur.* What do you need?'

Camus thought for a moment. By activating the *haut niveau* French government operational emergency protocols as he had already in order to be extracted from the crash scene he had raised himself and the DGER right up the flagpole into the light of day. Doubtless the Spanish would be asking some very hard questions of French embassy staff later today in Madrid. It was fortunate that his Beretta had been thrown clear in the crash and was nowhere to be seen; that would have been - embarrassing.

He would in any event be subject to half a dozen different types of audit and inquiry when he returned to Paris. A preliminary report of his extraction and the circumstances surrounding it would be landing on a desk in the Élysée later today - if it hadn't already. If he had to explain himself empty-handed, it would be the end of both his career and his agency. If, however, he came back with the goods, his fortunes would be transformed. He knew he had no choice. Stand as a wolf, or be hung like a baby lamb. *En avant...*

'When we land I need a new 'phone - and a van. A panel van. Nothing showy. A Bipper would be ideal.'

A pause. '*D'accord, Monsieur le Directeur*. You will be met. The items will be provided as requested. Will there be anything else?'

'No. Not from you. That will be all.'

Camus terminated the call and focused his attention back inside the cabin. One of the soldiers sitting opposite betrayed a flicker of emotion. It was the one with the French shoulder-patch. Camus eyed the machine pistol slung on a short sling across his chest, the barrel pointed safely to the floor.

'MP9?' He said, in an almost conversational tone.

'*Oui.*' Pause. 'MP9*N*' Another man of few words.

Camus was well aware of the weapon though he had never live fired one. The Brügger & Thornet MP9 was a Swiss-made machine pistol, the *choice du jour* of Special Forces units and SWAT teams across Europe. Compact, reliable, and very deadly. It's small size made it easily concealable. Funny, he thought, how a nation of habitual neutrals and *chocolatiers* consistently produced some of the most well-made, efficient - and expensive – portable killing machines on the market today.

'Give it to me.' He held out his hand. Both soldiers and the loadmaster tensed. The French soldier made no move to comply.

'Do as he says.' The pilot again, over the intercom. 'We have our orders. I will file the necessary report.'

Slowly, reluctantly, the soldier unshipped the B&T from his shoulder harness. Camus watched intently as he unclipped the long 30-round polycarbonate magazine and replaced it with a much shorter one - 15 rounds? - from a chest pouch. He slid it into the receiver with a snap and handed the weapon over, barrel downwards.

'One in the chamber. 15 in the clip."

"Merci. Good thinking on the smaller clip. Easier to conceal, eh?'

The soldier's face was impassive.

'You can do less damage with fewer rounds.'

'*Vive la Republique...*' said Camus, softly.

--o-0-o--

Andre Lucas drummed his fingers on the desktop. Ravi Bhindra, one of his most useful contacts "upstairs" had run an Investigatory Powers request on his behalf, pulling the mobile 'phone records of his two suspects. Bowman was in the clear - at least as far as this matter was concerned. However there were a number of anomalous calls and a whole raft of texts at odd times. Lucas studied the spreadsheet of call and text data on his laptop screen once more and frowned. Bowman might not be "consorting with agents of foreign powers" but he certainly appeared to be doing consorting of a different kind.

Lucas' problems did not end there. He readily recognised the other number as that of one of his own team; an experienced, well-liked and trusted operative by the name of Beth Shepherd. The call and text pattern was obvious - as was what was almost certainly going on. Whilst not a crime as such, it was a bloody stupid thing to do for both of them. It compromised Bowman's integrity and reflected badly on both him and Shepherd.

Deep down, Lucas also had a personal issue with the morality of Bowman's actions.

He was no angel himself but he was a man of firm convictions and took a dim view of infidelity - particularly in the light of the behaviour of his own - now ex- wife. Lucas knew full well that Bowman was married with a family and should, he thought, bloody well know better. He would have to speak to Bowman about it - in an official capacity - as well as Shepherd and he did not relish either conversation.

However that was tomorrow's problem. First he had to deal with Detective Sergeant Owen. The initial IP request didn't reveal any unreasonable or out of the ordinary activity on Owen's official issue 'phone but further cell analytics had thrown up an anomaly that Ravi had flagged for his attention. She seemed to have another 'phone, which always showed up in close proximity to the number they knew about. Again, that wasn't a crime in itself - Lucas carried a personal mobile of his own - but Owen only used this one to make and receive calls to and from a single mobile. A French number.

He sighed and unlocked and opened his desk drawer. It had been a long time since he had had to clean house. He pulled out his SIG Sauer P226 Elite, slid a 15-round magazine into the receiver and racked a 9mm parabellum round into the chamber before thumbing the safety. He reached into the drawer again and fished out a paddle holster into which the SIG smoothly slid. The holster sat comfortably on his hip as he shrugged into a well-worn Barbour jacket, long enough to conceal the sidearm.

Lucas checked the personnel file on his desk one more time, and punched Owen's home address into Google Maps on his 'phone. It had been a long time since he had last been to Streatham and he wasn't looking forward to it. But Owen had questions to answer, and time was of the essence.

One last call. After a moment's thought he hit speed-dial #3 on his own mobile and waited patiently while the call connected.

'Morning Boss. What's the word?'

'Day-word is "bookshelf". I need you to accompany me on a house-call. Draw a personal weapon and meet me in the car park. And Shepherd - keep this to yourself.'

'Sir.'

Lucas headed for the door.

Chapter 19

Guy winced with every step as they made their way onto the platform at Avenue del Alijarafe in Palomares del Rio. It was further and had taken longer than they had expected to walk but they were here now. The M-153 train would take them some of the way, but the station attendant they had found told them that they would have to change at Cuidad Expo and San Bernardo to get to the Santa Justa stop in the centre of Seville. It should take them about an hour, he said. The platform was crowded with commuters and students heading into the city and they made their way to the far end where they hoped that they would stand a better chance of finding a seat.

When the train pulled in Guy didn't argue when Almu quickly boarded first and shoo'd a couple of college-bound teenagers away from a double seat they were just about to grab. One turned to argue but she waved at the limping old man behind her with his walking staff and let loose a stream of what sounded to Guy like some particularly blunt Spanish. The kids backed off and Almu took his arm as he lowered himself into the not particularly comfortable seat with a grateful sigh.

'Are you in pain?'

'You could say that. My knee is knackered and this bloody pole has blistered my hand now. I've already got a blister on my left big toe from walking awkwardly and that's flared up again.'

Almu jerked a thumb towards Guy's backpack.

'Don't you have some painkillers in there? You seem to have most other things.'

Guy managed a wry smile. 'Good point. Yes I have some Ibuprofen, and another plaster or three.' He rummaged for a minute and pulled out the two packets from a side pocket. Almu handed him a small bottle of water and he grimaced as he washed the tablets down.

'Child.' She said as he handed the bottle back.

'Ah shut up. How long again until we change trains?'

'About ten minutes, I think.'

'Right.' Guy straightened in his seat and nodded towards the small toilet at one end of the commuter train carriage. 'Needs must. I'll check my toe while I'm in there.' He fished again in the pack and pulled out his X-Pro2, slinging it around his neck as he stood.

'What are you doing with that?' Said Almu in surprise. 'Take selfies in the toilet?' One of the teenagers still standing close by giggled and she shot him a dirty look.

'No, I was just going to use the time to make sure it was still working. It's been in two car crashes, remember?'

'You English are really weird sometimes.' She shook her head. 'Just don't be long.'

'No, "Mum".'

Almu stared out of the window at the increasingly urban landscape as Guy made his way past a number of morning commuters to the on-board toilet. She put his pack on the seat beside her to ward off any attempts to take advantage of his temporary absence.

She watched out of the corner of her eye as Guy closed the door and the red "ENGAGED" light illuminated. She gave it thirty seconds then reached into her own pack and pulled out her mobile. Her thumbs flashed across the keyboard as she entered a short text message. She read it back before hitting the "SEND" key.

"Approaching Seville. Fully trusted."

In the small toilet cubicle, Guy stood and looked at the camera in his hand. He had brought it with him having noticed the "WiFi On-Board" symbol in the carriage near where they had sat. He switched it on, activated the WiFi connection again, flipped the view mode to the rear screen and put where he could see it on the small shelf beside the sink.

He wasn't sure quite how the "revised" firmware that had been installed without his knowledge actually worked, but he certainly hadn't had to do anything special to have his viewfinder invaded by Bowman back in Lisbon so it was reasonable to suppose that all he had to do was turn the thing on within range of a router.

While he waited, he pulled off his shoe and sock and examined his sore toe. As he thought, the blister that had developed on the first day in Lisbon looked a lot angrier than before. He peeled off the little plaster with a grimace and used the sharp blade on the small Swiss Army knife on his keyring to relieve the pressure then cleaned it up with hot water and toilet tissue and applied a new, larger Compeed dressing with a sigh of relief. He sat and stared at the blank camera screen as he waited for the plaster to stick. Nothing. Perhaps the wi-fi wasn't working on this train - typical. It was just like South West Trains back at home.

At least he'd tried, thought Guy. He reached over and picked up the X-Pro2 to switch it off again. He turned it to one side and opened the side flap, to peek in at the two SD cards mounted inside. So much fuss over something so small, he pondered. The tiny micro SD card in the adaptor in slot 2 was still his responsibility to deliver and he took such things very seriously.

He glanced at his watch; he had just under an hour and a half now before the Seville rendezvous.

It was in the Cathedral de Sevilla, in the centre of town. The trains they were taking would take them as far as Santa Justa station and it would be a short cab ride from there.

He slung the camera around his neck and gingerly put on his sock and shoe again as he felt the train decelerate. Almost simultaneously, he heard a knock at the door. Almu.

'Come on, Guy. We have to get off soon.'

Guy washed his hands and opened the door. His foot felt much better and the painkillers had started to kick in.

Almu stood in the narrow corridor, Guy's pack slung over one shoulder, her own bag over the other and his monopod in hand. He took back his things and braced himself against a handrail as the train pulled into Cuidad Expo-Metro.

--o-0-o--

Camus watched as the helicopter rose into the sky from the car park where it had dropped him and turned away to the South. Standing beside him watching it go was a young, nervous looking attaché fresh from the office of the French Consulate General on Plaza de la Santa Cruz. He looked dishevelled and unshaven and frankly too young to be representing his country in any respect. Camus looked him up and down and held out his hand.

The attaché stared at it blankly then suddenly realised what Camus wanted. His hand dived into an inside pocket of his jacket and he handed over a brand new iPhone. Camus turned it over in his hand; he detested Apple - another big American company that thought it knew best - but it would do for now. Attaché Junior fumbled in another pocket and produced the keys to the nondescript dark blue Peugeot Bipper panel van parked a short distance away. Camus took them without a word and walked toward the van. Behind him, the attaché cleared his throat, nervously.

'*Monsieur*, I need to return to the Consulate…'

'That's your problem, *mon ami. Adieu.*'

Camus dropped his bag on the Bipper's passenger seat, settled himself behind the wheel and keyed the ignition. The satnav on the dashboard sprang to life and he took a moment to type in the location of the Cathedral de Sevilla.

A green line showed him the direction and a small readout showed that it was twenty minutes from his current location. That would do nicely. He turned on the iPhone and dialled a UK mobile number. The call connected but for a few seconds nobody spoke. Camus waited.

'Who is this?'

'Ruth, *ma petit, c'est Leon.*'

'Leon! I didn't recognise the number. What's happening? You intercepted Miller in Lisbon, as planned, yes?'

'No, Ruth, I didn't. Well, I did, but he proved more resourceful than I had allowed for. I am still on his trail, though, thanks to you. I am in Seville. I will intercept him again once he has made the second pickup. Although it is not as I originally planned it will work out even better, I think. But, my darling Ruth, I need you to help me. I need some back-up insurance, just in case. I need you to look after Mrs. Miller for a short while - just a few hours, until I am sure that I actually have the dispatch this time.'

'Leon… what do you mean "look after"? What do you mean? I'm not in this to kill anyone.'

Camus smiled thinly. Ruth Owen was of limited use. He had always known that. He wasn't surprised that she was equivocating now.

Back when the DGER had a sensible budget, it had been a simple matter to put the disaffected young Welsh police officer on the payroll. Her birth father, Ivan Owen, had been an active member of the militant Welsh nationalist group *Meibion Glyndŵr* and was arrested in 1989 for setting fire to a couple of cottages in the Brecon Beacons belonging to wealthy English weekenders.

An innocent young child had died in one of the cottages - the daughter of the owners. It had made headlines, including the fact that he had a one-year-old girl of his own. Ivan had never seen his daughter grow up; his wife divorced him soon after his conviction and he died in a prison disturbance in Parkhurst in 2005.

Ruth had been raised by her mother, who had taken her to live in London with her new English stepfather. She had proven a bright and motivated student, joining the Metropolitan Police and rising to the rank of Detective Sergeant before transferring to Special Branch in 2014.

Nobody in all that time had picked up upon the hatred that burned in her heart for those she saw as responsible for her real father's death - the English judges and the legal system that had put him in prison. It had not taken Camus' people long to find her, lurking in internet chat rooms. But they had warned him from the outset that she was long on bluster, and short on action.

Sensing a future use, Camus had taken on the task of grooming her personally as a covert source of information. He flattered and flirted with her, always tantalising and keeping her just the right side of committed as he spun her tales of how strongly he felt about her and the extent to which the world would be better if the English were put in their place. A proud and free Wales would be able to prosper in it's own right and she would be lauded in time as one of it's founding heroines, perhaps even with him at her side.

She had swallowed it all, hook line and sinker and had fed him and the DGER snippets, dribbles of sensitive information for years, in return for the occasional snatched afternoon together in a hotel and funds paid into a discreet little offshore bank account in her name.

Camus had been delighted when she had been seconded to the Queen's Wayfarers - he could not have asked for anything better. But he knew that she had her limits and balked at any thought of actually getting her hands dirty; she was a hypocrite, mused Camus - she didn't care if her grubby little actions led others into harm's way but she had no intention of pulling any triggers herself.

Well, she might just have to.

'Ruth, it is just this one thing you must do for me. It is very, very important. I need you to go to the house of Guy and Jane Miller. Go straightaway, and wait there for me to call.

You do not need to hurt her, as such. Just - detain her. Restrain her for a few hours, until I have concluded my business with her husband. If I do call you it will simply be for you to confirm to him that you have her and that you are *prepared* to harm her if he does not co-operate with me.'

Camus took a deep breath and moderated his tone, still speaking quickly but lowering his voice and adopting a more gentle manner. 'Ruth, Ruth, this is *so* important. We are so close to something that will change everything for ever. I will look after you, Ruth. I promise. I will personally welcome you to France as a heroine of the Republic and in time you will return to your homeland as a heroine there too.' Camus stopped talking and waited. He could hear Ruth breathing at the other end of the line.

'You'll get me out? This will be the end of my career…'

His tone hardened again. 'Your career working for the people who killed your father, Ruth. Never forget that. This is your chance, your time to strike back. Have your revenge.'

'Alright, alright. I'll do it, but I'm not going to hurt anyone for you or for anything.'

You won't need to actually harm Mrs. Miller, Ruth, just *sound* as if you are. Just… frighten her a little, so that her husband is convinced.

You are my insurance policy, Ruth - please don't let me down.'

Ruth Owen's voice sounded very far away. 'Ok Leon. And I will see you soon?'

'Oui ma petit. Very, very soon. I promise.'

Camus dropped the iPhone back on the seat beside him, glanced at the satnav and put the Bipper in gear. Now for Miller.

--o-0-o--

In her small one bedroom flat in Streatham DS Ruth Owen put down her mobile with a sigh. She knew that there was a possibility that one day she might be called upon by Leon to do something unsavoury but she had genuinely thought it would never actually happen.

She thought about walking away from her life - not much of a life, really - a small flat, no relationships that she had been able to sustain beyond a year, a mother who was always just a little too busy to make time for her and a career that she had to admit had started well but stagnated a few years ago. The burning anger that she felt about the unjust treatment of her father by the English establishment was her one remaining motivation.

How fortunate it was that Leon had come into her life, the day they first "met" online. She had felt so isolated up until then, but he had helped her to feel better about herself, given her purpose and – surely, in time, his love. At first he had been so caring, so supportive, so lovely. She would do anything for him, for just another few hours in his presence, in his arms. Well, almost anything.

She had thought that the oddly-worded secondment opportunity that had presented itself might re-energise her career but all that had happened was that Leon had changed his attitude towards her. He had become cold, less accessible and started to pump her for more and more information, while spending less and less time with her. She had fed back to him the movements of the Queen's Messengers at every opportunity, hoping it would bring him back to her. He had never seemed to do anything with the information - until now.

It wasn't all bad, she mused. In the process, she had accumulated nearly a million Euros tucked away in an offshore account. She had never touched it, never been near it, but it was there and it was hers. It would fund a new life for her wherever she wanted, particularly if Leon could help her to establish a new life.

She liked him; she trusted him, up to a point. They had met in Paris and in London more than once and he had always made her feel special.

He was older than her but had a certain Gallic charm that had always appealed to her.

Ultimately, she had concluded that he looked on her as just a pawn in a game, but pawns could have fun too…

Except this was not fun.

She had never met Jane Miller but had heard Guy talking about her one day in the coffee bar in the Queen's Wayfarers offices under the Palace of Westminster. She sounded like a nice lady; funny, warm, kind and resourceful. The sort of likeable person that Ruth always wanted to be and had never quite managed.

She stood and straightened, then picked up a stool from the breakfast bar and took it into the bedroom. She used it to reach up onto the top of her wardrobe. In a small black messenger bag were her passport, a few thousand in Euros and Sterling, a change of clothes and the unmistakable shape of a compact Glock 26 wrapped in clingfilm.

That had taken some getting. Another Special Branch officer had lost her sidearm during a shout and then lost her job in the subsequent board of enquiry; nobody had suspected that DS Ruth Owen had been responsible for the disappearing firearm.

She unwrapped the Glock and dropped it back into the bag; she didn't intend to use it, just to frighten Jane Miller with it. Only for a few hours, then she would leave her tied up and head for the nearest port and out of the country. She opened a couple of drawers and stuffed in a few more clothes; she had no idea how long she would have to travel for. She watered her spider plant, took one last look around the flat that had been her home for the past six years and walked out for what she knew was the last time.

Chapter 20

The connecting metro they had caught from San Bernardo pulled into Santa Justa right on time. Guy and Almu disembarked along with a horde of commuters, students and other travellers heading into central Seville for the day. Guy stopped for a moment and looked around; the city held good memories for him. He had last been here a few years ago during Semana Santa, shooting the Easter celebrations. It was a big thing for the city and the crowds had been ...memorable. The other thing that made Seville stand out, in Guy's book, was that it was the nicest smelling city he had ever visited; the multitude of orange trees that lined so many of the streets filled the air with a heady aroma in the springtime.

Sadly, this particular morning Santa Justa smelled pretty much like every other station in every other European city - an unpleasant mix of oil and grease, fast food, garlic and body odours. He smiled ruefully and followed Almu down the platform to the main concourse. His blistered toe was behaving itself and even his knee felt a bit better for not having been walked on too much for the past hour or so. He took stock of the bustling concourse then pointed at a small coffee bar.

"Would you mind just nipping over to that eatery - grab us a bite to eat and a couple of coffees, please.'

He handed Almu a 20 Euro note against her protestations and pointed at a left luggage office a little further on. 'I'm going to dump my backpack in there; I want to travel light for the next part of my journey. I can always come back and pick it up when all this is over.'

Almu nodded and headed off. Guy watched her go then picked his way through the crowds to the left luggage counter. He extracted the Hadley Pro containing his camera and lenses from the backpack along with a light windcheater and a cap, swapping them for the jumper he was wearing.

He hadn't mentioned to Almu the other reason for wanting to dump the backpack at this point - he wanted to change his outward appearance as much as he could; he didn't doubt for a moment that - if he was still able, following that crash - Leon Camus would still be in pursuit; the man appeared obsessed. Thus he felt that if there was anything he could do to give himself an edge, he would do it.

He had one more rendezvous to make, then he had to get himself back to the UK. Again, he already had a flight booked, this time from the airport just outside Seville back to Gatwick and safety, but again he was loath to make the connection given Camus' proven knowledge of his movements.

But that was a future problem.

The more pressing one was what to do about the young Basque girl who had been his companion for the past, eventful 24 hours. She had proven surprisingly helpful thus far; more so than he had any right to expect, or to ask.

They were in Spain now. He recalled that Almu had mentioned she had family in Seville; she could tie up with them now and be safe; Guy was confident that they would help to get her home in one piece. He would complete the rest of his journey on his own and would take great pleasure in getting back to London and shoving the micro SD card he was carrying up Bowman's nose - he hadn't signed up to be mugged, involved in car chases (and crashes) or shot at by lunatic French government agents.

Guy paid, took the key he was given and put the backpack in locker 217. The Billingham went over his shoulder. For a moment he considered collapsing the monopod and leaving it behind too, but then thought better of it - his knee was still tender and he didn't know how much more walking he would have to do; it might still prove useful.

He made his way back to the coffee bar and joined Almu at a small table she had managed to grab near the door. She pushed a plate with a sugary pastry in front of him and nodded toward a cup of intense black coffee.

'That's yours. I've finished mine already.'

She waited politely while he hungrily tucked into the pastry then leaned forward in her chair.

'What now, Guy?'

He licked his fingers clean of cinnamon-flavoured icing sugar and took a swig of the coffee before replying – partly to buy time while he marshalled his thoughts to get the words right.

'I'm glad you asked. This is where we part. Almu, I'm incredibly grateful to you - it's fair to say that I wouldn't have got this far without your help - but I can't prevail on you any further. I'll go on from here on my own. You can hook up with your local family, and get yourself home safe.'

Almu looked downcast and sat for a long minute before replying. 'I understand. I really do. I have enjoyed our little adventure, Guy. I thought I would just be meeting you to learn how to take better pictures, but all this…! The story I have to tell!' She grinned for a moment then looked serious again. 'But you are right, I know. I'll call my cousin and go and visit him, then I will go home.' She shrugged, and swilled the dregs in her own coffee cup for a moment before straightening up. 'Well, you are in Seville, as you wanted. Where do you go next?'

'I have to meet a …friend, at the Cathedral.' He glanced at his watch.

'In fact, I'd better make a move now - I need to be there in less than an hour and they are expecting me.' He stood and held out his hand. 'Be safe, Almu - and thank you.'

Almu stood too and started to take his outstretched hand, then stepped forward abruptly and threw her arms around his neck.

He stiffened at the unexpected embrace then gave her a big hug in return. She stepped back and looked at him with a frown. 'Be safe, Guy. You are a good man. Get back to England, go to your wife and tell her from me to take good care of you.'

Guy broke into an embarrassed grin, shouldered his bag, pulled his cap down low over his eyes and headed for the taxi rank on the station forecourt. Behind him Almu sat down again and watched intently until he was out of sight then pulled out her phone and dialled a number. She spoke rapidly, in Basque as she twirled a coffee stirrer between her slender fingers.

'Joni - Almu. Pick me up as quick as you can from Santa Justa station. We are going to church.'

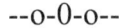

Joni Robles put down his phone and gathered his thoughts. They were few in number and it didn't take long. Almu had always been his favourite cousin; they had grown up not far from each other and had played together as children.

He had always had a soft spot for the bright young Almu – she was a couple of years younger than him but academically a lot brighter. As they grew up the age difference ceased to matter, but their paths in life diverged rapidly as Joni dropped out of school then drifted into a series of dead-end jobs and finally into petty crime.

He had grown up big, strong and fast, so it wasn't long before he found himself working as a "debt collector"; ever more frequently he collected more than money when the hapless debtors could not pay. Joni had found his niche – he discovered that he genuinely enjoyed hurting people; the longer he could make the pain last, the more he enjoyed himself. In time, he had made a name for himself as a man not to be crossed; indeed people went out of their way in Donostia to stay out of his way.

Life was good for Joni, for a while. He had money in his pocket and he engendered fear in others – which he mistook for respect. It all went wrong for him when a girl was found in an alley behind a club. She had been brutally raped and beaten and left for dead. With the active support of her parents and a shocked and disgusted local community she named Joni as her attacker and he found himself on the run.

He had taken refuge in Seville, and had lived there now for a little over a year. At first it had been really hard but then one day a man had approached him in a bar and sounded him out about his political inclinations.

Never one to worry too much about such things before, Joni was nonetheless intrigued by the sound of what the well-dressed, black haired man was offering; a steady job with a regular income and all he had to do was the occasional act of violence against someone who, he was assured, richly deserved it.

Life was good once again, and it got better when one day a couple of months ago his cousin Almu had called him out of the blue and told him that she had joined the same people. He dared to hope that it might mean they would see each other again, maybe even renew their friendship – and more.

Her last call to him had been yesterday; she had warned him to prepare himself; others were travelling South to help, she said and he would be needed. If he did well, she continued, she would be so grateful. He grinned at the thought and checked the magazine on a Beretta before tucking it into a shoulder holster. He made one call of his own and fifteen minutes later was in the back of a van headed at speed to the station at Santa Justa.

--o-0-o--

Jane Miller had awoken early as usual. The cat saw to that. He had no regard whatsoever for the fact that she had only had a few hours of disturbed sleep. Now fed, he had headed out on the endless quest for mice, birds or anything else that was smaller or slower than he was.

She stood in the kitchen dressed for work with a mug of hot black coffee in her hand and contemplated both the front garden and the day ahead. If all went according to plan, Guy should be back home tonight, or by the morning at the latest. She had made her mind up. She really didn't like his new job and was going to tell him so.

Working for the Queen's Wayfarers wasn't like the Queen's Messengers, at all. She didn't like the secrecy, she didn't like the unpredictability and above all she neither liked nor trusted Roger Bowman; there was something about the man that she found unpleasant. She and Guy would have to have a serious conversation on his return - after she had made him fully aware of how much she had missed him.

She started to turn away from the window but a small movement caught her eye. A silver car had driven slowly past a couple of minutes ago. She had idly noticed it. The road they lived in was a cul-de-sac, with only a couple of houses further up the lane past their own. It wasn't one she recognised as belonging to the neighbours - perhaps an early visitor.

As Jane watched, a crouching figure dressed head to toe in black curled cautiously around the yew hedge at the entrance to their drive then moved quickly off to the side, behind a camelia bush that Jane had been nagging Guy for years to grub out and get rid of. It was big enough to provide a lot of cover to anyone who felt the need.

It was only about 30 yards from the gate to the front door and there was a clear gravel path all the way - a path that the figure seemed not to want to use. Jane stiffened at the sight of the unexpected visitor and put down her coffee cup slowly and carefully.

The normal postman was a tubby, greasy-haired bloke with halitosis, prone to wearing shorts in all weathers, not a short, lean, black-clad man; he didn't move like someone trying not to be seen - and the postman carried a big red bag, not what looked very much to Jane's untutored eye like a pistol.

Chapter 21

Andre Lucas and Beth Shepherd stood tense and alert either side of the front door of Ruth Owen's flat. Both were armed, and each had their pistol at the ready in a double-handed grip, one in the chamber, safety off and barrel pointed to the floor. Lucas had briefed Shepherd in the car on the way over and neither was in the mood to take chances.

There were no sounds from inside. They exchanged glances and Lucas nodded once, curtly. Shepherd changed her grip and knocked briskly on the door with one hand. They waited. No response. Adrenaline pumping, Lucas waved Shepherd back a little and stepped back a couple of paces himself before aiming a hefty boot at the door, right beside the lock.

The door frame splintered and succumbed at the second kick and Shepherd immediately led the way into the small lobby area, her own SIG held up in front of her in a modified Weaver stance - ready for anything. She checked the door to her left - bathroom - then one to her right, a couple of paces on - bedroom. She couldn't help herself as she snap-judged Ruth Owen's taste in decor; it ran to pink, chiffon voiles and fairy lights above the bed. Little girl syndrome, she mused, as she called back over her shoulder to Lucas.

'First two rooms - clear.'

He stepped through the shattered doorway and advanced, his firearm at the ready. The door straight in front led into a lounge diner. It was for the most part tidy, but there was a jacket slung over the back of one of the chairs at the table, a couple of letters and a free newspaper beside a half empty coffee cup and a pile of what looked like gym kit, emptied out of a bag on the floor nearby. He quartered the room as behind him Shepherd passed through an arch into what was obviously the kitchen. Nobody there either. Still alert, she felt the electric kettle. Warm. A faint smell of toast hung in the air and a loaf of bread was spilling it's contents on the worksurface.

'Not long gone, Sir, judging by the kettle. An hour at most.'

Shepherd walked back into the living room where Lucas was standing. He had already holstered his SIG. She safetied her own and slid it into a well-worn tactical holster at the small of her back with a soft snick. Lucas was thinking fast.

'Check the bedroom, that desk over there, anywhere else likely. You're looking for her purse, wallet, phone, credit cards… and passport.' As he spoke he noticed something on the arm of the sofa, half hidden under a couple of magazines and a TV remote. It was a phone identical to his own. He picked it up and switched it on. Locked, as per policy. Ravi would be able to help with that, once they got it back to the office. He held it out for Shepherd to see.

'She left her work phone. Look for anything else useful - something that might tell us where she is.'

Shepherd moved to comply. Lucas pulled out his own phone and redialled a familiar number.

'Ravi? Andre again. You know that second mobile that showed up as being used by Ruth Owen on the IP check? Yes, that's the one – non work. I need to know where it is - now.'

Shepherd called to him from the bedroom. From the look of the drawers she hadn't hung about. He noted the stool by the wardrobe and raised a quizzical eyebrow. On top he could see a somewhat battered, bright pink wheelie suitcase and what he thought were a couple of hat-boxes. In between was a gap.

'No sign of passport, Sir.' Shepherd pointed to a drawer half open. 'There's a folder in there with a confirmation and ticket to Crete - hotel in Aiya Napa, dated first two weeks in July.'

Who'd have thought it? mused Lucas. Our Ruth at a foam party... 'Anything else?'

Shepherd had climbed on the stool and was examining the top of the wardrobe. 'From the dust up here - she was no domestic goddess - something has gone, just recently. I'd say a small case or more likely a soft bag - edges aren't clearly defined.'

Lucas' phone vibrated.

He looked in irritation at the screen then his face cleared. He answered the call.

'Ravi? This is quick, even by your standards. What can you tell me?'

The frown returned as he listened. He looked at Beth as he listened, his eyes hard. He terminated the call with a swift 'Thank you kindly.'

'Call the office. Get Romano and Barratt down here to secure the place. Then fetch the car while I call the police. We're going to Farnham. Now.'

--o-0-o--

Guy paid the taxi driver and looked in awe at the massive bulk of the Catedral de Sevilla. It loomed in front of him across the square where he had been dropped. It was a big bugger, he thought; bigger than he remembered and certainly more imposing even than St Paul's in the City of London. He vaguely recalled reading somewhere that it was the largest actual cathedral in the world; he wasn't in the mood to argue.

He resisted the urge to dig out his X-Pro2 and take a shot or two; he didn't have a real wide-angle with him

- plus there was the little matter of focusing on the task he was there to accomplish, not on the scenery for once.

He sighed in mild frustration and started forward, feeling a bit like a medieval pilgrim with his monopod "staff" in his hand.

His rendezvous briefing for Seville was straightforward; be in front of the tomb of Christopher Columbus in the cathedral at 11AM, no more, no less.

He cast another hard look around, in the guise of framing up another shot or two of the cathedral exterior and plaza. The last he had seen of Camus was as his car spun out on the motorway but the man seemed to have nine lives and a direct line to his future movements so it made sense to be wary.

He glanced at his watch - 10:45. Time to pay the 9 Euro entrance fee, get inside and find the tomb. Having been there before he at least knew what he was looking for; a gaudy extravagance borne on the shoulders of four men, somehow fitting for the last resting place of the old colonial chancer.

Guy dodged his way around a couple of school parties and a tour group - Russian from their dress and what he could hear of what their guide was saying - and bought his ticket from the little booth. He used his official issue credit card again - he was beginning to think of it as a calling card. The interior of the cathedral was cool and smelled faintly of incense. It was enormous – cavernous even; the sense of scale somehow greater on the inside than out; a sort of oversized ecclesiastical TARDIS.

As he walked along one side of the marble-floored nave, past the odd *Sevilliano* at devout prayer he looked around him at the opulent carvings and stained glass. His X-Pro2 was around his neck now, in full tourist mode. The monopod in his hand made an irritating click each time he put it down on the hard floor so he loosened off the leg locks and collapsed it, stashing it for now just under the lid of his Hadley Pro. He left the locks loose in case he needed to put his weight on it again in a hurry.

If anyone asked, Guy tended to describe himself as an "antitheist" - one step beyond an atheist. In general he regarded himself as about as religious as a cheese roll; about the only source of friction in his marriage to Jane, who enjoyed the odd hour in a church doing the praying thing and was active at their local church. Guy admired the architecture, and particularly the human ingenuity and effort that went into the construction of places like this, and of course a good sing song at Christmas, but that was where it stopped for him.

He watched as a little old lady with an ornate black shawl over her white hair went to a stand and dropped in a coin to "light" a votive "candle". The little amber led bulb even flickered - a nice touch, thought Guy with a trace of cynicism. He missed the old candles; the warmth and the smell of the tallow, not to mention the challenge of hand-holding at $\frac{1}{8}$sec to get an evocative low light shot. Progress, eh? He wondered how long it would be before the candles were lit by an app...

Guy shook himself out of his reverie, pulled back his sleeve and checked his watch. Four minutes to eleven. About 50 yards ahead he could see the dull glint of silver, illuminated by the light from the great stained glass windows to his right. He waited for a couple of nuns to scurry across his path, each carrying a heavy looking basket of flowers and made his way to the tomb of Christopher Columbus.

The tomb was as he remembered it. Imposing and more than a little over the top. He looked around but could see nobody who looked even vaguely like a contact - but then the lady behind the counter hadn't exactly looked the part either... He made a mental note to himself to be a bit more observant of people - nobody thus far on his journey had turned out to be what they seemed - except Almu, of course. Poor kid - he hoped she was safely on her way home by now.

Guy mooched about for a moment or two, then mentally shrugged and decided to make the best of his time and snap the tomb.

He dropped the Billingham at his feet, swung his X-Pro2 to his eye and framed a tight shot of the face of one of the pall-bearers.

'*Ola, Señor.* You like our little monument to Christopher Columbus? You know, there is some doubt he is actually inside?'

He lowered the camera slowly and turned to his left. Beside him stood a silver-haired priest in a smart black suit, his hands clasped behind his ramrod-straight back and a heavy silver cross around his neck.

Guy looked more closely. The apparently austere priestly garb was just a little too well tailored to be official-issue. A hint of ivory lining showed near the high collar and the sleeves were the perfect length. The fabric too looked a lot more upmarket than the norm, with a subtle twill twinstripe weave. His hair was a little on the long side, but beautifully cut. His shoes were polished to a high shine. "Not a hair out of place." Guy's old mum would have doubtless said. Overall the new arrival looked sleek, monied. A contradiction in terms, surely?

Guy nodded slowly in greeting. 'Padré...'

The elegant cleric turned now to face him. His eyes peered bright and shiny above a pair of rimless spectacles perched low on his aquiline nose.

'The carving is very fine, would you not say?'

'It's not to my taste I'm afraid. I prefer modern art.'

The priest nodded, gravely. 'Enough small-talk, I think. You have something for me, Mr. Miller?'

Guy was a bit more on the ball this time.

The code phrase used by the priest was correct and he in turn had - immediately this time - given the proper response; the one that indicated to the contact that he was acting of his own free will and not under any duress.

He looked around him then flipped open the side flap on the X-Pro2 and extracted from it the SD adaptor containing the micro SD card. A moment of fiddling with a thumbnail and he had the tiny card given to him in by the tea lady in Lisbon in the palm of his hand.

He held it out to the priest who took it carefully and slipped it into a small mobile device that he had produced from an inside jacket pocket. He waited patiently for a moment as the new media was recognised then opened a document upon the screen, scrolled to the last page and studied it with a grunt of satisfaction. Guy watched as he touched a couple of buttons and selected "Add" from a pull-down menu. A progress bar started to crawl across the screen.

They waited in silence for a moment before Guy spoke.

'Nice day for it.' He said, conversationally. The priest raised an elegantly manicured eyebrow in surprise; the first emotion he had shown.

'You are remarkably calm, considering the significance of your task, Mr. Miller.'

'Padré, yesterday I was threatened, robbed at knifepoint, chased, involved in two car crashes and shot at. I haven't had a decent cup of tea in 72 hours. I assure you I am not calm, I simply have no adrenaline left.'

The priest smiled slightly and returned his attention to the screen on the device in his hand. As he watched, the progress bar moved from 95 to 98 per cent, then finally showed complete. He entered a couple more commands then cut and pasted a second file on to the Micro SD card from his device. Finally, he ejected the card and passed it back to Guy.

'It is done. The electronic signatures on the first document are now complete, and there is a "bonus" as we promised your superiors as a gesture of the good faith of my principals.' He straightened and brushed imaginary dust from his elegant jacket.

'I shall pray for you, Mr. Miller. The future of Europe itself is now in your hands. Treat it well. Much depends upon the success of your endeavours. *In nominae Patris, et Filii, et Spiritus Sancti...*'

He blessed an uncomfortable Guy with the sign of the cross, turned and made his way smoothly around the vanguard of another tour party that was just coalescing around their guide in front of the tomb of Columbus. He was gone from sight in a moment, leaving only a faint trace of expensive aftershave to mark his passage.

Guy was jostled from one side by a teenage girl in a thick puffa jacket; it was unintentional, he realised - her attention was glued to the screen of the oversized iPhone in her hand - but it almost caused him to drop the precious Micro SD card. He gripped it firmly between finger and thumb and headed across the nave to somewhere a little less well populated.

He found himself a pew in a quiet side chapel and sat down for a moment. It was an ornate shrine to the Virgin Mary. Guy couldn't help but feel that the blue and white robed figure with hands outstretched glowered down on him disapprovingly. He turned the tiny SD card over in his palm and prodded it about with his little finger. So small, and yet so important...

He pondered his options for concealment; he could put it back in the camera, but he had pulled that stunt once and he was loath to try it again. The priest's words echoed in his mind - "The future of Europe is now in your hands. Treat it well." It sounded like pretentious nonsense to Guy, but he felt that he shouldn't take any chances.

He sat back in the pew and shuffled his feet; as he did so his blistered toe reminded him of its continued presence with a nagging twinge.

He gingerly slipped off his shoe and sock and examined it. The Compeed plaster he had applied on the train was still in place, stuck like a limpet.

From past experience it would stay there now until he either peeled it off or it fell off, it's job done. As he studied his toe, the glimmer of an idea formed and he reached into his bag to find more plasters.

--o-0-o--

Outside the Catedral de Sevilla, Leon Camus sat in the dark blue Bipper van and looked out over the plaza. Off to one side the carriage drivers were doing a brisk trade, with eager tourists queuing for a short ride around the town's historic centre, having the sights spoon-fed to them.

Generally he detested tourists; they were for the most part cultural imbeciles. They looked but they did not appreciate. Most of all he detested the modern cult of the selfie - it reminded him of a proof of life, with a hostage holding up a newspaper with today's date. It seemed in today's society a simple photo of something was not enough - you had to get yourself in the shot to prove that you had really been there.

On his way to the Cathedral, he had appropriated a couple of "props" to make himself and the van blend in. He smirked at the thought – had not Miller himself written about being ignored because you looked like you belonged there? Just in front of his bonnet he had positioned a set of well worn cones and barriers surrounding a cracked paving stone.

They bore the figure-eight wool-skein symbol of Seville's municipal authority. Ten minutes ago they had been arranged around an unattended pothole in a quiet road three streets away before he had pulled up and quickly loaded them into the back of the Bipper. Now they gave him and the van a reason to be there.

His blinking hazard flashers completed the fiction; he looked vaguely official therefore to all intents and purposes to the casual observer, he was official.

He knew his hastily improvised subterfuge would not stand up to any real scrutiny - the cracked paving slab he had spotted as he pulled up was a bonus - but was a flimsy excuse that would not fool a police patrol or even a real council workman, should one show up.

The B&T MP9 nestled under his jacket. He could feel it's cold weight against his ribcage, still sore from the battering it had taken in the car crash. He sipped at a cup of coffee and gingerly fingered his cut and bruised face. He had caught sight of himself in the Bipper's door mirror earlier; he looked like a prize fighter, albeit one who had lost the bout by a country mile. Another thing Miller would pay for, he mused as he took another sip and studied the crowds of locals and tourists emerging from the Cathedral in a steady stream.

He had positioned himself directly opposite the main exit and had a clear line of sight of everyone who stepped out blinking into the bright sunlight.

His plan, such as it was, was simple - Spot Miller, threaten him with the gun, get him in the back of the van and take him somewhere quiet, where he could take his time to ...extract... yes, extract - the card. Camus did not think of himself as a violent or vindictive man but he felt that he had every intention of making sure that Guy Miller would have ample reason to remember his name.

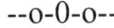

A few minutes later Guy emerged through the great door of the Cathedral and paused for a moment at the top of the steps to get his bearings and to scan again for any sign of Camus. He planned to head back to the station and pick up his things from the left luggage store then go and check into a nearby hotel to clean up and get a few hours of sleep.

While there he would sort out safe passage home; he was thinking in terms of another train journey, to either Santander or Bilbao in Northern Spain - from there he could hop on a ferry as a foot passenger and get back to somewhere on England's South coast - Portsmouth maybe, or Poole; either would do. It would be a simple matter to get from there on to London and relieve himself of his dispatch.

He looked warily around at the plaza in front of him. He could see knots of tourists, taking snaps, checking maps, listening to guides or just generally milling about.

A gaggle of schoolchildren, noisy and excited, were being herded in his direction by a couple of exasperated looking teachers and a nun. Over to one side of the plaza, in the welcome shade of some trees were the horse-drawn carriages lining up to take couples for a ride - in more ways than one, Guy thought with a wry smile. A modern tram hummed past on the other side.

The sun warmed his face as he stood there and he slipped on a pair of sunglasses. He caught sight of a stand of taxis, waiting for their next fare. He thought about un-limbering the monopod again to help him get down the steps but decided against it; his knee was behaving itself, for now. He started down the steps unaided and made his way in the direction of the cabs, jinking slightly around a small van and a coned-off area of pavement.

'Why Guy, we meet in the most unusual places… You have mislaid your resourceful little girlfriend, I see.'

The driver's door of the van opened and Camus stepped out. He moved slowly and seemed to be clutching his side – injured perhaps, in the crash? As he stepped around the front of the van he let his hi vis jacket fall open to show the malevolent dark shape of the machine pistol concealed within. A flip of his thumb, a soft metallic snick, barely audible in the big open space and the safety was off. The stubby barrel pointed directly at Guy's solar plexus.

Guy was irrationally annoyed at the sight of the Frenchman. He took some pleasure in the obvious battering that he had taken since they had last been face to face but it was nothing compared to the anger that was welling up inside of him.

'Fuck *off* Camus. I have had just about enough of you. You aren't going to use that thing here - even you are not that stupid.'

Camus narrowed his eyes and tightened his grip on the MP9. 'Why Guy, you are not pleased to see me? I thought you might react more favourably to a familiar face, so far from home.' He shrugged, then winced slightly as he did so. 'It is of no matter. Rest assured I *shall* shoot you if you give me any reason to do so. I have no qualms, and nothing to lose.'

He pulled out his phone from his jacket pocket. 'Plus, I have a – I think you say "ace in my hand"? I have a very special friend back in England. She is - let us say - "visiting" - yes, visiting - your wife, as we speak. One word from me and... pouf.' He dropped the phone back out of sight, opened the back doors of the van with one hand and motioned with the barrel of the MP9 into the darkened interior. 'Now Guy, give me that bag and get in the back. *Allez!*'

Guy stiffened. He weighed the odds. Camus was armed, with something that looked like it could cut him in half. From the look on his battered face he was just crazy - or desperate - enough to use it too.

The immediate threat to himself was clear. The additional implied threat to his wife might be real, it might not... Camus could be improvising to destabilise him. He knew he should comply with the Frenchman's demand, to be on the safe side. But he was tired. Tired of being threatened, tired of running, tired of playing whack-a-mole with this seemingly irrepressible French bastard.

Not far behind him, Guy could hear the unruly schoolchildren being scolded and cajoled by their teachers, and their laughter and squeals of delight at being out of class for the day. He felt the breeze on his face and caught the faint aroma of horse manure from the carriages off to one side. In the distance a siren wailed, ululated then faded into the distance, away from the plaza. Time, for just an instant, slowed to a crawl.

He had two options. Get in the van, without making a fuss, or make a stand then and there and stop Camus' nonsense once and for all.

On a sunny day in Seville, Guy Miller chose the latter.

Chapter 22

'Sir. Miller has completed the second rendezvous.'

Bowman put down his coffee and crossed the Ops Room to stand behind Linda DiSanto. She pointed at the screen in front of her which showed a graphic workflow of dark blue boxes with white text, with Guy Miller's name at the top right. The last two entries, date and timestamped, told the story – the credit card he carried had been used at the cathedral in Seville and shortly thereafter there was a one-line entry in a box of a different colour – this time pale green:

"Met Miller. Transfer completed. *Ve con Dios.*"

'Thank f.... goodness for that.' Bowman glanced at DiSanto and moderated his language – she was only young, part of the recent staffing up exercise. He straightened and read the last line again.

'Any idea what that last bit means in English?'

DiSanto nodded. Her grandfather was Spanish. 'It means "Go with God", Sir.'

Bowman sighed. 'He can go with Ryanair, for all I care, as long as he gets back in one piece. Thank you Linda. Keep monitoring. Report any further indicators.'

--o-0-o--

Guy stood still and waited. Camus was standing close - just a few paces away - either through inexperience or over-confidence. As he considered the possibilities, Camus even moved a half step nearer, impatient for Guy to do his bidding and trying to apply pressure by doing so.

What he actually did was improved the odds in Guy's favour – very slightly. He looked around slowly, trying not to make any sudden movements that would make Camus pull the trigger. There was nobody near, no possible source of distraction, or help.

Make a decision.

He shrugged in apparent submission, shifted his weight onto his good leg and eased the Billingham from his shoulder with one hand. It started to drop as it left his shoulder and he reached around quickly with his other hand as if to steady it. The grip of his monopod was sticking out from the lid and he grasped it tightly as it came to hand.

The weight of the bag kept it falling to the ground and he whipped the monopod under the lid out and around as it did. With the leg locks already unfastened, it extended rapidly to it's full five feet with a series of metallic snicks as he brought it around and up in a backhand arc.

The steel tip of the foot cracked hard up against Camus' cheekbone and he gasped in pain, momentarily caught off-guard.

Guy followed through by using his momentum to step inside Camus' reach then drove upward with the heel of his hand against the Frenchman's chin as with his other hand, still holding the monopod, he smacked down hard to deflect the barrel of the MP9.

Camus stumbled backward but kept his feet under him by leaning up against the side of the van. The sudden change of fortunes caught him by surprise and his finger tightened reflexively on the trigger. A sound like ripping wet cardboard rent the air and in under a second the short magazine was empty, the rounds tracing a sparkling line across the flagstones of the plaza.

Senses heightened, Guy heard the sudden screams and the sound of running feet. He shifted his grip to press home his advantage but it was too late. All pretence of subterfuge a thing of the past, Camus regained his balance and lunged at Guy with all his own bodyweight, hurling the now useless machine pistol to one side.

The fast counter-attack drove Guy backward and he tripped over the Billingham, hitting the ground hard, winding himself.

Camus straightened, took a fast step forward and aimed a vicious kick into Guy's left kidney, sending fire coursing through his side. He rolled away from the attack and into a ball as much out of instinct as intent as he struggled to get his breath and get back on his feet.

Neither noticed the two large Mercedes vans that bumped over the kerb and headed rapidly in their direction as Guy turned to face Camus again.

The Frenchman had pulled out his knife and was advancing rapidly, the sharp blade held point down and edge forward, ready to slash and stab. In the distance sirens started again as word of shots being fired in front of one of the great European centres of Christian worship triggered an immediate top level terror alert.

Guy scrambled to put some distance between himself and the gleaming knife blade as he looked for an opening to once more regain the upper hand. He had managed to keep hold of the monopod and now raised it straight up. The sections compressed quickly once again through gravity and with one quick movement Guy locked them together. He now had a short stick, a little over a foot long, that he could use at a pinch as a club - if he could get close enough to do so without being caught by Camus' blade, now moving in lazy figure eights as the Frenchman advanced.

They were suddenly bracketed by the two Mercedes vans, as they pulled up tight around the two men to form a triangle with Camus' much smaller Peugeot. The two larger vehicles screeched to a halt and doors opened. Several masked and armed men emerged from one to join them in the centre of the triangle.

Guy looked at the guns in their hands. Czech Skorpions. Small, deadly, reliable, capable of easy concealment and rapid fire - but quite venerable now, and not used by any modern security forces. More the choice of criminals - or terrorists.

Guy couldn't help the untimely thought that he was outgunned by just about everybody he met at the moment.

One man, smaller and slighter of build than the others, stood off to one side. He waved a gloved hand and one of his associates levelled his gun at a spot between Camus' eyes before speaking.

'Drop. Now.'

Camus seemed as surprised by this turn of events as Guy himself, he noted. The Laguiole dropped to the floor with a metallic tink. Apparently not DGER backup then. A third party? He let his own hands hang limp by his sides, trying to work out what was going on while trying not to make matters worse. The police sirens grew ever closer.

Shorty didn't seem unduly perturbed. He nodded towards the Bipper. The one with his gun trained between Camus' eyes spoke again.

'Hands on the side of the van. Both of you. Now.'

His accent was Spanish, to Guy's ear. Home grown terrorists? Local criminals? Every bugger seemed to want a piece of him today.

He turned slowly and complied. Beside him, Camus did the same. There was a movement at his back - and then sudden stifling darkness. A thick black bag was pulled over his head and a drawstring tightened roughly around his neck. Guy fought a rising tide of panic, but realised that the cord had been pulled tight enough only to prevent him shaking the bag off.

Hands gripped him by the shoulders and he was spun roughly around. His own hands were pulled in front of him and he felt cable tie cuffs bite hard into the flesh of his wrists. Beside him, judging by the noises and protestations Camus was getting the same treatment. Guy was manhandled in the direction of the second Mercedes van and found himself dumped face down in the loadspace. A soft thump and a theatrical moan led him to think that Camus had joined him a moment later.

Doors were slammed and the Mercedes vans peeled out of the plaza via the Avenieda de la Constitucion just before the police arrived.

The captives were thrown from side to side as they negotiated the twisty streets of the old town.

It was an uncomfortable ride as the big vans threaded their way through pedestrians and market stalls, turning and braking sharply, blasting their horns to clear their path.

A Guardia Civil Toyota Landcruiser suddenly appeared from a side turn and gave chase, siren wailing and blue lights flashing.

The lead van, carrying Miller and Camus, accelerated hard but the second dropped back, allowing the Land Cruiser to make ground.

When they turned down a particularly narrow alley, the second van suddenly slammed to a halt. As the Land Cruiser slewed to a standstill behind it the back doors of the van flew open and the malevolent snout of a .50 cal Browning M2 machine gun came into view. Behind it sat a man in a balaclava, with another at his side feeding in a belt of ammo. He lowered his aim and opened fire straight at the Guardia Civil Toyota.

The officers flung open the doors and dove for cover as the front of their 4x4 was chewed into sparking fragments by a hail of automatic fire and the vehicle exploded into a fireball, it's heat triggering secondary fires all around.

The doors on the Mercedes shut again and it accelerated off after it's twin, leaving mayhem in it's wake.

They drove for what felt like hours but was probably only a few minutes. The vans turned into a large underground car park and stopped beside a smaller and newer Mercedes Vito minibus, its windows darkened to the point of opacity. The men piled out and retrieved Guy from the floor of the first van.

Guy felt himself manhandled into a seat in another vehicle and a lap belt being fastened across his hips. At least they didn't intend for him to die in a crash, he thought with a grimace – he was touched by their consideration. He was jostled as another body was dumped into the seat beside him.

Camus? He couldn't tell.

Standing beside the Vito the group of men quickly removed their balaclavas and overalls to reveal casual street clothes. They threw everything into the back of one of the vans before most left on foot back the way they had driven in a few moments before.
Handshakes and hugs said their goodbyes more eloquently than words.

Three of the group stayed behind, including the short one that Guy had noticed in the plaza seemed to be in control. They worked quickly, dousing the vans and all their contents in petrol before setting light to them.

As the flames took hold one slipped into the driver's seat of the Vito while Shorty and another got into the back, in seats facing Guy and Camus. The driver started the engine - a surprisingly throaty burble gave notice that the engine under the bonnet had been breathed upon by Mercedes' AMG special vehicles subsidiary; clearly this was no airport taxi.

Guy was thrown about in his seat as the Vito accelerated up the ramp and broke back into daylight. Sirens could be heard all around as the Seville police and Guardia Civil tore the city apart in the hunt for the terrorist suspects responsible for the shocking events at the Cathedral less than an hour ago.

Guy bided his time. There was little else he could do, blinded and bound.

Sharp twists and turns soon gave way to smoother progress and it was apparent that they were on a motorway heading out of town. Beside him Camus shifted uncomfortably in his seat and Guy himself tried to stretch out his legs to ease the cramp that was threatening to grip his calves.

'Guy? Are you there, *Mon ami?*'

'I am NOT your friend, you tosser.'

'We are in the same... boat? - is that right?'

'We are in the same vehicle.'

He paused, listened. He could hear nothing beside the noise of the engine. 'Who *were* those people? Friends of yours?'

'They are definitely no friends of mine. I work alone, these days.' Guy thought he detected a note of irritation in Camus' voice.

'You lie. You said you had a "friend" in England, with my wife. Or is that a lie too?'

Guy felt a movement against his shoulder as Camus shrugged wordlessly beside him.

'It is no lie. She should be with your wife now. If you did not co-operate immediately I would have...'
'You would have WHAT, exactly? What is WRONG with you? You harm Jane in any way and I will break every bone in your nasty little body, Camus. Do you understand?'

Another shrug. 'I understand, but I think you are in no position to make such a threat, Guy.'

Guy started to respond, but was stopped in his tracks by a light touch on his knee. At first he thought he had imagined it but there was clear pressure for a moment – almost a squeeze – before the hand moved away again. Abruptly, the hood was removed. Even behind the smoked glass in the back of the Vito, Guy was momentarily blinded.

He blinked rapidly and spared a glance at Camus who was still hooded and oblivious to what Guy could see.

He looked across at the two people in the seats opposite - a man and a woman. The man was staring out of the window trying not to laugh. The woman had her full attention on him and was holding a compact Beretta - a PX4 Storm, by the look of it. Even though small, it looked large in her steady grip as she pointed it straight at his chest.

'Almu?'

--o-0-o--

Jane Miller had never regarded herself as a pushover. Her father had been a farmer, who hosted the local shoot on his land for many years. She had grown up around guns, often sitting in the warmth of the gun room snuggling up to one of her father's labradors while he meticulously cleaned his own shotgun after a day in the field. She had been brought up to respect guns, of all types. One of the first rhymes she had ever learned went:

"Never ever let your gun,
Pointed be at anyone.
All the pheasants ever bred,
Will not make up for one man dead."

She was eleven years old before she was allowed to shoot herself. Under strict supervision she was allowed at first to use a single shot, small bore shotgun of indeterminate age that her father referred to as "The Ratter". He kept it on a high shelf in the kitchen and went around the farmyard every so often with it himself taking pot-shots at the vermin that the cats either missed or wouldn't take on because they were just too large. She had learned quickly and was a natural shot.

After the death of her father in later years she had given up live birds, but along with Guy she kept her hand in with sim, or skeet shooting, up the road from where they lived at a club just across the border in Hampshire.

They had a couple of shotguns of their own, that they kept locked in the gun cabinet, bolted to the floor of the fitted wardrobe in the second bedroom. Guy favoured a Browning, but Jane's own gun was an over-and-under Webley 900.

She lay now in their bedroom, alongside the bed, on the opposite side from the door. It was too low for her to fit under, but she was well concealed from a casual observer. Her Webley was lying on it's side within reach under the bed, both chambers loaded and the barrels pointed towards the door. Her right arm was outstretched and her finger lightly on the trigger. She was trembling, and it wasn't just from holding the awkward position.

The intruder had lost no time; as she had rushed upstairs the dark figure had crossed the lawn to the back door and as she unlocked the gun cabinet she had heard the unmistakable tinkle of breaking glass downstairs. She forced herself to breathe deeply as she tipped out a box of shells and loaded the Webley, then moved as quickly and quietly as she could to her current hiding place.

Now she waited.

A creak betrayed the fact that the intruder was climbing the stairs.

She had nagged Guy for years about the loose fourth tread and he had jokingly referred to it as his "early warning system". With an exasperated sigh she realised that he was right – and that he would never let her live it down.

As long as she lived.

She stared under the bed at the bottom of the bedroom door. She couldn't help but notice the dust bunnies that seemed to be throwing a small party there; time for a thorough clean. There was that earring she had lost a few weeks ago, too - and Guy's Fitbit; she had bought him that for Christmas and he had claimed he had lost it.

Time to get a new cleaner...

She snapped back to the present as the door swung open a few inches. Her finger tightened slightly on the trigger; it was adjusted to her personal taste, with a slightly lower pull weight of 3 pounds or so.

All she had to do was curl her finger just a little more.

A familiar tabby face popped around the edge of the door. The cat spotted her instantly and headed under the bed with a self-satisfied "mrowp". The adrenaline dump nearly made Jane's head explode, as the cat rubbed against her cheek with a deep purr.

She moved her left arm to wave him away, but froze again as the door opened a little further. A black trouser leg came into view. The shoe was a flat, rubber soled trainer, also black. Quite small, Jane noticed, randomly.

She knew she had a fraction of a second before her hiding place was exposed - it would only take a couple of steps into the room. The second foot appeared beside the first. She visualised the intruder scanning the room for threats before entering further. A thought popped unbidden into Jane's mind; at least the bastard wasn't wearing steel toe caps.

She pulled the trigger.

The boom of the Webley was deafening in the confined space. The terrified cat effectively dematerialised as it fled the commotion. The gun bucked in her awkward grip and the shoulder stock smacked painfully against her collarbone.

The smell of singed carpet and obliterated dust bunnies was overwhelming in the confined space under the bed.

On the other side of the bed the intruder's feet and ankles were peppered at point blank range by lead shot. Jane was rewarded by a piercing scream as the intruder was flung off their feet by the blast. They fell forward, their head and upper torso hitting the bed, landing hard on their knees, writhing in agony.

Jane flinched as a pistol bounced to the floor just behind where she was lying concealed.
She scrambled to her feet and dragged the Webley out with her, pointing it unwaveringly at the groaning figure half on and half off her and Guy's bed.

A siren wailed in the distance as she carefully kicked the pistol to the far corner of the room. She still had one barrel loaded and was sufficiently fired up to use it if the groaning figure – a woman, she now realised, to her surprise – made any threatening move at all. It took her a moment to grasp that just wasn't going to happen.

'Got you, bitch.' Jane muttered softly, fighting hard to keep her voice level as the room was lit by the flashing blue lights of a police patrol car roaring up their drive.

Chapter 23

Lucas and Shepherd's car was halted by a PCSO a hundred yards or so from Guy and Jane Miller's house. The road ahead was blocked by a cordon of tape and cones not to mention a gaggle of police cars, an unmarked white van and an ambulance.

Lucas showed his ID and they were waved through. A police officer in a tactical sweater and a cap covered in silver braid was standing in the drive being briefed by a couple of junior officers and Lucas made straight for him.

'Andre Lucas. Cabinet Office.' He jerked a thumb. 'Beth Shepherd - she's with me.' The senior officer glanced at the pass he waved and registered an official looking card and a silver crown and compass embossed on a black background before Lucas stashed it again. 'We called you chaps in the first place. What's happened? Where's Mrs. Miller? Is she okay?'

The story that he had given when he placed the call from Ruth Owen's flat was that Jane Miller was the wife of a high ranking civil servant who had been threatened with serious injury by one of his colleagues who had suffered a nervous breakdown.

He had communicated enough urgency to have caused a local patrol car to be despatched.

The rest of the circus had turned up when the first officers on the scene had been let in by Jane with a broken shotgun over her arm and an automatic pistol held out delicately between thumb and forefinger like a dead rat.

She had shown them upstairs, where Ruth Owen still lay, moaning softly and curled into a fetal position in a state of shock. Her feet were a mess - a 12 bore cartridge at point blank range did that - and had lost a lot of blood.

Shepherd had hung back a couple of paces and was the first to catch sight of the paramedics as they emerged from the front door with Owen on a stretcher. A saline drip had been set up and her condition had been stabilised before being moved. The ambulance crew had pumped her full of morphine and as she was carried past she looked straight through Shepherd as if they had never met. Shepherd felt a moment of sympathy - but only a moment.

'Chief Inspector Iain Lefevre. Your lady is inside, in the kitchen. There's a WPC with her. She's shaken but unharmed; the paramedics checked her over. Looks like your ...employee broke in and threatened her with a pistol. She defended herself with a shotgun legally registered in her name. Funny thing - her assailant's not carrying any ID but there's a car just up the road registered to a Ruth Owen, who happens to be a DS with the Met...'

He leaned close, the peak of his cap almost touching Lucas' forehead.

'What. The. Fuck. Is. Going. On? This whole scene stinks to high heaven, along with your story. I have 20 years in the service and the only time I have ever seen a mess like this before some very funny people turned up and shut the whole investigation down as if nothing had happened. I don't believe you, I don't believe Mrs Miller and I don't take kindly to people pissing about on my patch.'

Lucas stood his ground without flinching. Lefevre was a type he had met many times before during his time in the Guards. Their hearts were in the right place but they liked order, discipline, predictability. They were hard to argue with, purely because they were absolutely certain that they were in the right. Always.

He met Lefevre eye to eye, unblinking. 'In a different life, Chief Inspector, you and I would be down the pub, drinking IPA and laughing about bloke shit. But we aren't. We're here. You know those "funny people" you referred to? Guess what? That's us. Immediately after this short and unremarkable conversation I'm going to go in to chat to Mrs Miller, while you and your boys and girls toddle off about your business catching sheep rustlers and graffiti artists, or whatever passes for crime around here.

Within the hour, Chief Inspector, your Chief Constable will receive a call from a man I report to.

This whole thing will melt like a Calippo dropped by a careless toddler on a pavement in August.' He half-turned to Shepherd and caught her eye. He nodded towards the paramedics as they loaded Owen into the back of the ambulance.

'Take a ride with her, Beth. I suspect you'll end up at - Frimley Park?' He glanced back at Lefevre, whose eyes flickered uncertainly. '...Frimley Park. Call Romano. Get him to come down when he's finished at the flat and relieve you He can stay there until we can get the MoD police to take over. I'll come and pick you up myself when I'm finished here.' Shepherd turned on her heel and moved to comply. Lucas turned his attention back to Inspector Lefevre. His tone softened slightly.

'We're both on the side of the angels, Iain. I'm just a little closer to heaven than you. Let's do this the civilised way, eh? Thanks for your prompt assistance here today. We'll take care of things from now on.'

Lefevre was incandescent. He had not been spoken to in this way since he was a young constable in Merseyside. He drew himself up to his full height and snapped back at Lucas.

'I don't give a *toss* who or what you have on your side. Get it into your thick head that this is MY patch, MY crime scene and MY investigation. Now you have ten seconds to leave or I will arrest you and your little girlfriend. Do you *understand*?'

Lucas understood very well. He waited for a count of ten before taking half a step closer the senior officer and responding in a low voice. 'I don't have time for this testicle-wrestling, Iain. You won't do that, because when all is said and done you value your career. I can, with just one call, speak to people who will in turn ensure that you are clearing your desk this very afternoon and that your pension will be tangled up in internal investigations until the day you die. I trust I am crystal clear.'

All around the bustle of activity had died to silence. Out of the corner of his eye Lucas could see Shepherd standing stock still like everyone else, waiting for the battle of wills to result in a winner.

Chief Inspector Iain Lefevre hadn't risen through the ranks of Surrey Police without developing a keen sense of personal survival. He took a deep breath then nodded once more and turned to a hapless constable - the nearest within range - and started barking orders to pack up and move on. Lucas left them to it, turned on his heel and made his way up the path to the front door. He followed his nose to the kitchen, where he found Jane Miller busying herself pouring hot coffee from a filter jug for a slightly bemused looking WPC.

'I don't think you'll have time to finish that. Your boss is packing up. I'll look after Mrs. Miller from here. Thank you kindly.'

The WPC looked from one to the other and seemed about to dispute the abrupt dismissal when the young officer that Lefevre had dumped on outside stuck his head around the door and jerked it in an unmistakable "follow me" motion. She left, shutting the door behind her and Andre Lucas turned to face Jane Miller.

The stinging slap was the last thing he expected.

Jane Miller went up a couple of notches in his estimation. Not only had she bagged a half brace of armed intruder, she hit like a pro. He rubbed his reddening cheek and pulled up a chair.

'May I sit down?'

'Have I a choice? I assume you are one of Bowman's lackeys. You can pass that on.'

She sat down abruptly. Lucas noticed the tremor in her hand as she gripped her own coffee cup. She stared at him with tears forming in her eyes. Delayed shock.

'Mrs. Miller, I'm Andre Lucas. I am Head of Safety for the Queen's Wayfarers so yes, I do report to Roger Bowman. I deeply regret what has happened here today…'

'Regret? *Regret?* Mr. Lucas, you have no idea.

My husband is messing about somewhere on the continent thanks to your Mr. Bowman. He mentioned some "French interference" when he called me last night. I know full well something is not right. Now that woman breaks into our home – our *home* Mr. Lucas - with a gun. God knows what she intended. It's not on. I hold Bowman responsible for all this and I will blow his top secret old boy's club out of the water if my husband does not come home safely - am I clear?'

'Crystal clear, Mrs Miller.' Lucas had been unaware that Guy Miller had been in touch with his wife - until now. He wagered that Bowman didn't know either. 'It's my job to help get our Wayfarers home. It's a job I take very seriously indeed. If your husband needs our help to get over the line my team and I will act. He will come back to you in once piece. It's what we do.' Lucas' phone vibrated at that point. With an apologetic shrug he pulled it out and glanced at the screen.

"Miller made Spanish pickup. Bowman."

He put it screen-down on the table in front of him and turned back to Jane Miller. A large tabby entered via a catflap in the back door, bounded up onto Jane's lap and was now staring at him with a furry frown. Jane was stroking it soothingly but it didn't seem to be doing much for it's mood - or hers.

'Your husband is an experienced and resourceful man, Mrs. Miller; we would not have recruited him otherwise. I cannot discuss operational issues but I can tell you that to the best of my knowledge he is still en route as planned.' He tapped the back of his phone. 'I have just had confirmation that he is in Spain now and has completed that leg of his journey. He just has to bring his dispatch home now. I am sure you will see him shortly. I suspect he is sipping a coffee outside some cafe as we speak, planning his trip home.'

--o-0-o--

Guy was not interested in coffee at that moment. In fact there was little that held his attention beyond the gun that Almu levelled at him.

'Please - point that thing in another direction. I really don't want to be killed by a pothole.'

Almu smiled thinly and crossed her arms, thereby pointing the PX4 at the door beside her.

'Same old Guy.'

'I'm not likely to have changed - I only said goodbye to you a few hours ago. You on the other hand seem to have acquired some ugly friends since then.'

The man beside Almu stiffened visibly and turned to face Guy.

Before he could retort Almu laid a hand on his arm.

'This is Joni. He is one of my cousins. He speaks good English. He also has a very short temper. Please do not upset him.'

Guy nodded to face him. 'Hello Joni. I'd shake your hand but that's a little difficult at the moment.'

Joni grunted and turned back to the window. Beside Guy, Leon Camus shifted in his seat.

'What is going on?'

Joni reached across and ripped off Camus' hood. Before he stopped blinking he was rocked back in his seat by a fast punch. Blood started to seep again from his bruised lip and he shook his head, spraying crimson drops around the cabin.

'That is for scaring my little cousin in Portugal.' Joni growled. He reached over and took the Beretta from Almu. 'I will not hesitate to shoot you, French. You are not part of the plan. If it was my choice I would push you out of the door now. Almu told me to bring you along - she did not want to leave you for the Spanish police to find. If you want to live, keep very still and very quiet.'

Camus nodded slowly. 'You have the gun. Under the circumstances I will concentrate on the fact that I am alive for now.

I would like to stay that way.' He tilted his head back and sniffed heavily, dabbing his lip with his sleeve and appeared to focus his attention at the landscape flashing past in a blur.

Guy turned his attention back to Almu. 'Would you like to explain just what is going on?'

Almu crossed her legs. 'Of course. We have some time - and a long drive ahead of us. Make yourself comfortable and I will tell you what you want to know.'

Chapter 24

Beth Shepherd sat at Ruth Owen's bedside and turned her phone over and over in her hand. She hated hospitals, ever since she had spent too much time in one on her abrupt and unscheduled return from Afghanistan. The ugly white scar tissue that marred her left shoulder itched when it was going to rain; it was more accurate than any weather forecast. She would have gladly swapped her new-found precognitive powers for not having the flashbacks and nightmares that plagued her most nights.

Her convoy had been ambushed by a Taliban cell; a firefight had ensued and a stray round had penetrated both the door of the Land Rover she had been sitting in and the body armour she was wearing. She was evac'd later that same day, just another casualty of a dirty little war.

The irony was that in spite of her military police background and training she was - technically - a non-combatant that day. She had been in country in an advisory capacity, working with the British Army. Her employer at the time had been very solicitous, very caring - and very keen to keep the whole thing quiet; it was the very body armour that had let her down that they were keen to sell to the Army as part of a multi-million pound procurement; it was designed specifically for women, and intended to be light, tailored and above all, safe.

They had paid her off handsomely, in return for her not making a fuss. She had had the best of private medical care and physiotherapy, taken the money, bought herself a small two bed cottage in the New Forest and set about rebuilding her life. She had heard about the Queen's Wayfarers through a friend of a friend and within months found herself a member of, not just an elite team, but a family.

She straightened in the uncomfortable seat; the thin back of the chair pressed awkwardly against the SIG holstered at the base of her spine and made it difficult to find a position that worked for long.

She reached out towards the table by the bed then stopped. The plastic cup of barely drinkable machine coffee was cold; it made it no more unpalatable than it was already but she was no masochist. Beth sighed - Owen was still - apparently - asleep. Sedated. But she could not leave until she was relieved. Romano still hadn't arrived; his apologetic texts explaining how bad the traffic was on the A3 didn't help.

Her thoughts turned to Roger Bowman. He had not texted her at all today, which was unlike him. She tried to kid herself that they were not having an affair, but all the evidence, she recognised, was to the contrary. It was true that they had not actually been to bed together since that night in Gleneagles, but he was persistent to the point of recklessness. She felt guilty that she had sent mixed signals, both in Scotland and since.

The fact that she knew one of the most powerful men in the country would do almost anything to have her again was a powerful drug. She felt conflicted, torn, between the desire to be desired and the need to keep her life on track – it had taken her a long time to get herself back on an even keel and she knew full well that she was gambling with her future every time she texted him back.

Beth studied the figure on the bed. A frame had been put under the blankets to raise them away from Owen's heavily bandaged feet. A heart-rate monitor beeped softly and a drip ran from a saline bag to a cannula on the back of her hand. Her breathing was deep and even. A steady stream of oxygen was being supplied through a nostril clip.

They were in a secure room off the main ward and Beth could hear voices in the corridor outside - normality, distinct from the bubble in which she found herself. Right then, she hated Owen. Hated her for betraying the Queen's Wayfarers, hated her for betraying her country and most of all hated her for destroying trust within the team.

They had never worked together; Owen's role was domestic, Shepherd's mostly extra-territorial - but she had seen her around the offices on occasion. Ruth had always struck her as cold, distant - she didn't mix with her or with the other members of Andre's team - perhaps now she started to understand why.

Behind her she heard a heavier footfall, stopping outside the door.

She rose quickly from the chair and unholstered her SIG, gently thumbing off the safety. The door opened and Andre Lucas stepped in, pulling it to behind him. Shepherd exhaled slowly and lowered her pistol.

'Boss...' She nodded to him. He acknowledged her with a smile.

'Staff nurse tells me that she's not going to be in the market for a pedicure anytime soon.'

'No. Apparently she was lucky not to lose more than one toe. The trainers she was wearing took some of the blast, but the surgeon had to spend a lot of time picking leather and shot out from the wounds. Mrs Miller did a thorough job.'

Lucas shrugged. 'No sympathy. Has she shown any sign of waking?'

'Not at all. Romano's delayed...'

'...I know. I "delayed" him.'

Beth stiffened.

'Beth, I need to talk to you. The investigation that turned up Owen's anomalous behaviour shed light into other - areas. What you might call collateral intelligence…'

Beth said nothing. There was nothing to say.

'Beth. I can't have secrets in my team. We have to trust each other - without doubts. Is there anything you would like to tell me?'

Silence.

Lucas glanced around the room then took the chair and lowered himself into it. Beth remained standing - there was nowhere else for her to sit - or hide.

Lucas waited. He had time. The silence was punctuated by the periodic beep of the monitor.

Beth Shepherd felt trapped. Her mind in a turmoil. She was very, very good indeed at compartmentalising her life into neat, self-contained parcels and suddenly one part of it had smashed into another. She knew Andre Lucas well enough to know that he would not let it lie.

'It's nothing. Really nothing at all. I…'

'Bullshit. Have another go.'

Beth stepped to the window. It was part frosted, but she was tall enough to look over the opaque panel. She could see the helipad on the roof of the building opposite and the air ambulance helicopter parked there.

The last time she travelled on in a heli she was being airlifted to hospital in Helmand, with bits of kevlar and a 7.62mm slug embedded in her shoulder. She chose her next words very carefully indeed.

'I have done nothing wrong.'

'Legally, no. Technically, possibly. Morally...'

Beth turned to face Lucas.

'Boss. Andre... I spent just one night with Roger Bowman. A few weeks ago, when Barratt and I provided close protection for him at the conference in Gleneagles. It wasn't intentional, and it didn't continue.'

Lucas snorted. 'Remind me to re-issue guidelines on what constitutes "close protection".' He snapped. 'Do you need your head read, Shepherd? How the hell did you think it would turn out?'

'I didn't. Think, I mean. Not at the time. We both knew it was wrong, but it happened.

It wasn't planned. We agreed afterwards that it was stupid - terminally stupid - and we've kept away from each other since.'

'But you have stayed in touch. Sometimes up to a dozen texts a day. At all hours. For weeks. Discussing the weather? The price of diesel?'

'We just talk. Talk. That's all. Roger's an interesting man. He listens. He…'

'…is MARRIED, Beth. Has a wife. Children. A big fuck off tabby cat. And one of the most sensitive jobs in the United Kingdom, particularly now. He is not free to flirt, or to provide ad hoc emotional support for one of his junior employees.'

Beth stiffened. Weeks of frustration, denial and subterfuge boiled to the surface. She stared down at Lucas and took a half step forward, her fists clenched in suppressed anger. All the emotional debt built up in the weeks since that night in the Spirit Suite boiled to the surface.

'It takes two to tango, Andre. Don't take it out on me. Roger's not a fucking innocent.'

'I know that. And I will talk to him too. It's my responsibility to do so. Anything that impacts the security of the Queen's Wayfarers is my concern. I was going to see him about this first, but this opportunity arose.'

He glanced at his watch. 'Romano will be here soon. I need to know two things, Beth. Right now. Honestly. One. Have you told me the absolute truth?'

'Yes.'

'Two. Will you stop?'

Long silence. Then Beth spoke, in a small voice. 'Yes. But you have to ask Roger the same question.'

'Oh I plan to. You could – probably will - both lose your jobs over this. And more.'

'I know.'

'One more thing. Does anyone else know?'

'No. Not even Barratt suspected, when we met at breakfast the next morning. God, that man's got the emotional intelligence of a used breeze-block. No, I haven't said a word and I'm sure neither has Roger.'

'I knew.'

Lucas and Shepherd froze and turned to the bed. Ruth Owen had opened her eyes and was regarding them both. They exchanged glances. Beth spoke first.

'How?'

Ruth licked her dry lips. 'Oh sweetie, you made it blindingly obvious.'
'Obvious? How?'

Ruth struggled to sit up. Lucas helped her into a sitting position while Beth stood and stared. Finally, Ruth continued.

'Ever since I joined the Wayfarers you came across as GI fucking Jane, little miss hyper professional, on a mission to prove you were better than the men; better than all of us, in fact. Then after Gleneagles everyone noticed you started wearing perfume, nail polish. You had your hair tinted.'

'So?' Lucas. 'What of it?'

'It meant that something had clearly changed in *her* life.' She pointed at Beth. 'Then one day I saw you hand Bowman a cup of coffee without him asking. It wasn't hard to put two and two together then. I'm a DS after all – solving crimes goes with the territory.' She smiled, then winced as her lip cracked. 'To be honest, I thought it made you a bit more human – just like the rest of us.'

A knock at the door broke the tension. Romano eased into the room, which was now starting to feel more than a little crowded. Hard on his heels was a nurse wearing a furious expression.

'This is a hospital, not a social club. We gave permission for one of you to be here at a time. Now it seems you are having a party. Two of you need to go. NOW.'

Lucas and Shepherd exchanged glances and headed out of the door.

Romano tried with limited success to make himself small in the corner of the room as the nurse bustled about checking the monitor readouts and the patient notes at the foot of the bed.

Ruth Owen watched them go, impassively. Out in the corridor, Andre Lucas turned again to face Beth Shepherd.

'This is a twenty-four carat mess.' He said, exasperated. 'It could – should – have been avoided. You are both old enough to know better.'

Beth shook her head slowly. 'She knew. She bloody *knew*. I - we were so careful - SO careful…'

Lucas looked her up and down. 'This isn't over, Beth. Not by a long shot. But just for now it's not my top priority. We have a Wayfarer inbound and it's our job to be on point to make sure he gets home in one piece. Go back to the office and await further instructions. Romano and I will have another talk with Detective Sergeant Owen.'

Chapter 25

Guy waited, impassive. Almu took a deep breath then began.

'We live in difficult times, Guy. The world is changing. You on your little island have been insulated from so much for so long you don't realise how bad it can get - actually, how bad it *will* get. Borders that have been stable for decades - even centuries - are not going to be there anymore when the dust settles. My people - the Basque nation - can see all this. We sit on one of the fault-lines of history, Guy - and we are not going to allow ourselves to be crushed when the earth moves.'

'You sound very much like someone I know.' Said Guy in a flat monotone. 'He talks just like you. What a pair of rays of sunshine you are. Tell you what, I'll put you in touch. He has some wonderful toys to help him make his points. You seem to have, what, a gun?'

'And a cousin.' Almu nodded to Joni, who remained impassive. 'And a family. And a movement. A cause. A people. A nation.'

'Yes, you touched on all that before, when you lectured me back in the Range Rover. All very passionate. But what are you expecting from me?'

'Guy, we know who you are, and what you are doing here. We know about the Queen's Wayfarers; we have done for hundreds of years. For many, many years the Basque people have been a friend to Britain. We worked with Wellington's Exploring Officers against Napoleon and again with your agents during the Spanish Civil War, together against Franco. We helped your SOE get British aircrews across the Pyrenees from the French side of the border into neutral Spain during the Second World War. We are your friends, Guy, for a very long time and we want to be treated by Britain as a firm friend in the new world to come.'

Guy held up his hands, still fastened by cable tie cuffs. 'You have a funny way of treating your friends, Almu. Did you read 50 Shades, perhaps?' Joni stiffened and leaned toward Guy with a low growl. He spoke to him for the first time.

'Don't talk to my cousin in such a way, English. She likes you. I do not. Remember that.'

Guy nodded slowly and sat back once more. No point in making matters worse - at least until he found out what was going on.

'*How* do you know, Almu? It was no coincidence or administrative cock up that led to you meeting me in Lisbon, was it? He raised his eyes heavenwards in frustration. 'How come every gun-toting bugger in the Iberian Peninsula knows about me? Was it posted on Facebook or something?'

'Not quite.' Almu smiled genuinely for the first time since they had reunited. 'It is actually a little ironic. We have a - friend - in the French government. She works as an intern in the finance offices in the Élysée. A few weeks ago she came across a workflow request from your French friend here; a justification for expenditure – a request for approval. It had apparently been refused once, so he had kindly provided more detail.

There was enough there for us to know who you were, Guy, where you were making your first rendezvous and at least some understanding of what you are carrying and it's importance. In particular we know that your Spanish contact in Seville was due to give into your safe keeping a list of French operatives in Britain, in order to buy favour with your government.

We want that list, Guy. We know how valuable it is to Britain, and how useful it will be in the months and years to come. We will trade it with your government in exchange for all that they can tell us about the *Centro Nacional de Intelligencia* and their covert operations against us in the very heart of Basque Country.

We know MI5 knows about this - your British Intelligence operatives have been all over their Spanish counterparts for years as part of your "insurance policy" for that insignificant little rock, Gibraltar.'

Guy was momentarily taken aback. 'You got on my case because Camus here put in a TRAVEL REQUEST?' He turned his attention on the Frenchman. 'And you - YOU were stupid enough to fill in a fucking form with all that you knew?'

Camus stirred. 'Not all, *mon ami*. But I had to get approval to travel, in order to come to meet you.' He shrugged. 'Bureaucracy, you see? We think we are in control of our own destiny but we are all simply at the mercy of the auditors.'

'This is beyond bizarre.' Guy shook his head. 'Are there *any* state secrets anymore?'

Camus answered, before Almu could say another word. He spoke quickly and kept a wary eye on Joni as he did so but the big man seemed preoccupied and kept staring at Almu. 'Guy, you have to understand - for years now all the European security services have intermingled and co-operated both overtly and covertly against our perceived common enemies outside of Europe - Russia, China, Iran, North Korea and more recently Daesh. It is very cosy.

Everyone drinks at the same bars, plays golf at the same clubs; there is even a secret service dinner every time those who call themselves "world leaders" meet at Davos. We work together, exchange intelligence, swap data on a regular basis. Freedom of information in exchange for restriction of freedom. We are all part of the greater Europe now.

It is what happens - and it is what is about to unravel if we do not stop what you British have started.

Most have almost forgotten how to keep secrets from each other or even how to compete on a national level. There is a whole generation in the intelligence communities who know other European nations only as allies.

Only a select few have maintained national interests against the tide and are ready for the change that is to come. I...' Camus drew himself up in his seat. '...I am one of those select few.'

'Oh shut up.' Guy growled.

Almu put a finger to her lips and Camus studied his fingernails. She continued.

'So you see, Guy, I am not your enemy. This man is your enemy. I mean no ill will to you, or to Britain; I just want to see my nation take its rightful place alongside yours as a part of the new European order and treated by Britain in the years to come as a valued equal. Do you not see that?'

'Don't make me laugh, Almu. You are just a terrorist by another name.' He turned in disgust to the window then looked back at her once more. 'What happens now? Where are we going?'

'We are headed to a safe house. Once we are there you will hand over the dispatch and we will hold you for a little while, as our guest, while we negotiate with your government.

Once they in turn have given us what we want you will be free to go on your way; in fact I will take you to the airport and put you on a plane personally.' She leaned close. 'Your time with us does not need to be unpleasant, Guy. Give us what we want quickly and you will be our honoured guest for a short while.'

Joni stirred once more and cleared his throat. '...and if you do not co-operate you will not be going home. Ever.'

A look of concern clouded Almu's face and she spoke quickly. 'Guy, you need to understand. My cousin is not a patient man. He - and others - believe that we have been too gentle with you already. I disagree - but for your own good you must help me. You must give us what we ask. Please.'

Camus snorted. 'A very pretty speech, *ma petit*. But I do not think that Guy is as stupid as you think he is.' He fell silent when Joni raised his hand as if to punch him once more. He growled at Camus.

'You, are a complication. If I had my way you would be dead already.' His eyes flickered across once more at Almu before he continued, then he spat at Camus' feet.

'But you still live. If you wish this to continue, French, I would keep very, very quiet if I were you.'

Camus smiled, a thin smile. 'I really should have slipped my blade between your pretty ribs when I had the chance, *ma petit*.' He never saw the punch from Joni that knocked him out cold.

Almu pulled Joni back into his seat, took a deep breath, smoothed her hair and composed herself. 'Now just sit back and relax, Guy. We will be on the road for a few hours yet.'

Guy shouldered the unconscious Camus off him and shuffled around in the seat to look out of the window at the countryside whipping past as they headed North on the E-803 in the direction of Salamanca.

Chapter 26

Andre Lucas sat in silence in the coffee shop in Frimley Park Hospital. He had downed a cup of almost but not quite coffee without really tasting it; a blessing in disguise. Now he sat munching on a warm Kit Kat as he gathered his thoughts before he went to talk to Owen.

What a fucking mess. By one brief indiscretion that laid himself wide open to blackmail and worse Bowman had not only blown his credibility but also likely ended his long and distinguished career, not to mention his marriage - and all for a fling. The fact that Owen said she knew just made things worse. Stupid, stupid, stupid. Nearly as stupid, in fact, as he realised he had been, raising the matter in the room with Owen present, even if she had appeared to be asleep.

He thought again about Shepherd. She was heading back to London now. He knew her background and had hand-picked her for his team; she had not put a foot wrong up to this point, quite the contrary. This was an aberration, a slip, but it put a massive great blot on her own previously exemplary record. He had yet to make up his mind; he would need to hear Bowman's side first - but he might have to dispense with her services too. A shame; she had shown great potential and was a well liked and respected member of his tight knit team.

He screwed the chocolate wrapper into a small ball and dropped it onto the empty cup, then headed for the lift. One of the advantages of Frimley Park was that it had a military wing, due to the close proximity of the army bases at Aldershot and Sandhurst.

The room in which Owen was being held was in that wing, which had the advantage of being both secure and relatively discreet. Lucas didn't have the manpower or the resources to deal with Owen as he would have liked but he had resolved to at least question her himself before handing her over to the MoD police for as yet to be specified offences under the Official Secrets Act, 1989...

As he approached the door a doctor in the day uniform of an Army Captain left the room in conversation with the nurse who had turfed him and Shepherd out earlier. He was intent on studying a sheaf of notes and barely noticed Lucas until he was right in front of him.

'Doctor... "Wood"?' Lucas peered at the name badge.

'Yes. And you are?'

'Andre Lucas. Ms. Owen is here under my authority.'

'Indeed.' The doctor's eyes narrowed.

David Wood was no fool, and not one to be intimidated. He looked Lucas up and down. The latter's casual clothes and appearance said one thing, his posture and direct gaze sent a different message.

'Is there any reason why I should not ask Ms. Owen some questions now, about what happened?'

'No medical reason. She is in no danger and her condition is comfortable. We have her on some powerful analgesics but they do not affect her lucidity.'

'Thank you.'

Captain Wood turned to go then paused. 'Mr. Lucas… This is all most irregular. I have a patient with shotgun wounds being kept at your express request in a secure room. You are not police - so what are you?'

'What indeed? Some days I wonder myself.
The MoD police will take over shortly, doctor. I just need one conversation with Ms. Owen.'

Wood stood his ground for a long minute and Lucas thought he might have to be more insistent. Then the pager on the doctor's belt beeped insistently and with a mutter of exasperation he handed the notes folder to the nurse, stepped around Lucas and left. She gave him a filthy look then made her way back to her own station.

When Lucas opened the door he found Owen still sitting up, propped by pillows. She looked drawn and white and the nasal oxygen feed was still in place. An ill-fitting hospital gown did nothing to make her look any more comfortable. She was sipping water from a beaker as he walked in. Romano sat in a corner with a newspaper. He looked thoroughly bored. Lucas had some sympathy; this wasn't the sort of work that he or his team had signed up for. Needs must, he thought, as he folded his arms and regarded the figure in the bed.

'Ruth. Let's start again. You know who and what I am?'

'Of course I do. Everyone in the Wayfarers knows you. They call you "Alfie".'

Lucas was momentarily nonplussed. In the corner he couldn't help but notice that Romano had raised the newspaper slightly so he could not be seen. A slight shiver of his hands suggested he was stifling a laugh.

'Care to explain..?'

'It was one of the girls in Operations. She went to see Les Mis. a while back and fancied you looked a lot like Alfie Boe. She thought it was particularly appropriate because he sings a song in the show called "Bring Him Home".'

Lucas regained his composure and ploughed on.

'Why were you at the Millers' house this morning with a gun?'

'If I tell you I will want something in return.'

Oh here we go, thought Lucas. This was not entirely unexpected.

'You are in no position to bargain, Ruth. We already have enough to put you in a very dark place for a very long time without your telling us anything more.'

Owen put the plastic beaker down and looked straight at him. She had had ample time to think and she knew she had little left to lose. 'Then why ask? You have no direct authority over me, Lucas. I'm on secondment from the Met. You and your toy soldiers have no clout here. I'm a trained and experienced police officer; I don't intimidate easily. I know I'm in deep shit right now, but I'm not saying anything - particularly not to you - without legal representation.'

She closed her eyes and laid her head back on the pillow. 'I'm tired now. My feet hurt. You are wasting your time. Tell your boss that he needs to pull some of those strings he is famous for and get me out of here - or he might find himself out of a job.'

Lucas shrugged. 'You aren't going anywhere Ruth, and Bowman's not going to do anything to get you out of trouble.

We have ample evidence that you have consorted with an agent of a foreign power. I have asked for a forensic examination of your finances – I'd be surprised if they turn nothing up. Above all we have the gun you took to Jane Miller's home this morning. Were you expecting a quick coffee and a chat?' He leaned closer. Romano folded the newspaper and laid it neatly in his lap.

'Just tell me one thing, Ruth. Why? Why betray your friends and your country? Is it the money? Are you that easily bought?'

Owen opened her eyes and looked at Lucas in disgust. 'You really don't get it, do you? You are a typical privileged English posh boy. I bet you've never had to work – really work – for anything in your life. You have no idea what it means to see people like you break up lives and families and keep whole communities in poverty just so you can go on bleeding us dry to fund your oh-so-perfect lives. You English make me sick.' She closed her eyes again.

Nonplussed, Lucas exchanged glances with Romano, who shrugged in confusion.

'"You English"? Is this something about your being Welsh? You are having me on. I thought all the animosity died when you were given your own regional parliament. What are you, a throwback? Good grief.'

A soft tear rolled down Ruth's cheek as she answered in a hoarse voice.

'No. I'm a daughter.'

--o-0-o--

The black Vito turned up a dirt track in the gathering gloom. They had been off main roads for nearly an hour now and Guy's back was feeling the strain, not to mention his bladder. He had slept on and off, as had they all, as the Mercedes chewed up the kilometres from Seville to Getaria.

Apart from a short refuelling stop, they had not paused and he and Camus had been kept in the van at the point of a pistol held in Joni's unwavering hand. Petrol station "refreshments" had been provided but they were close to inedible.

They had passed a sign some time ago that advised they were entering the province of Guipuzcoa, but that hadn't told Guy much.

They were bumping slowly up a dirt track now, hemmed in by hedges and featureless and uncommunicative fields. Joni had made a call a few minutes ago and relayed what was said to Almu. She stared intently at Guy for a moment or two then busied herself with her own phone.

Camus had regained consciousness from Joni's punch hours ago. He had made periodic plaintive requests as they drove - a cigarette, some water, a beer, another cigarette, his freedom - but everything had either been ignored or flatly refused. He had eventually slumped into sullen silence and seemed currently to be dozing, with his head lolling from side to side. He and Guy had to suddenly brace themselves as they ground to an abrupt halt.

Guy could see through the windscreen that they had come to a set of gates set into a white stucco wall. The wall was high, with pantiles along the top, suggesting some substance to it. The gates were wooden - solid, grey with age but still sturdy looking. The driver of the Vito sounded his horn; two short blasts then one long. After a pause, the gate opened and they edged into a large inner courtyard. A new looking Toyota Landcruiser stood off to one side under a low roofed car-port and two or three other cars were parked in a group near what looked like the front door to a large white building in the centre of the courtyard.

Guy guessed that this was the safe house that Almu had spoken of. It looked a bit like an overgrown Swiss chalet, with the same widely pitched roof and an exterior that suggested a timber frame and stone walls. Much of it was stucco'd like the outer perimeter wall but the corners showed bare stone, each one the size of a steamer trunk. The windows that he could see were small and set some distance apart.

Judging by those windows the building had at least three floors above ground, although the upper floor windows were close enough to the pitched roof that Guy suspected he wouldn't be able to stand up straight if he went all the way up.

The whole place looked to be a few hundred years old although it had clearly been modernised, as evidenced not only by the freshly painted walls and clearly double-glazed windows but also the aerials and satellite dishes, spotlights and surveillance cameras he now started to notice on the building itself and also on some of the surrounding outbuildings and even the wall itself.

The side door of the Vito was slid open from outside and a stocky man wearing a waxed jacket and pointing a Skorpion machine pistol waved them out. Camus and Guy disembarked, stumbling to keep their balance after so long cramped in the van. Almu and Joni followed and headed towards the main door as wax jacket man kept an eye on them. Guy noticed that Almu had retrieved his Billingham bag from the front passenger seat and had it slung over her shoulder.

Standing in the doorway at the top of a short flight of stairs was a tall man with thin features and a shock of dark hair that had started to run to grey at the temples. He wore leather breeches and a high-necked black waistcoat over a white collarless shirt. He turned his attention first to Joni whom he greeted with a firm handshake and a warm hug.

Almu received no handshake but the hug bestowed on her spoke of true affection. The three spoke for a moment in low voices then the man made his way over to where Guy and Camus stood.

'Welcome to Baserri Otxoa' he said in a warm almost accentless baritone. 'I am the *Etxekojaun* - you would say in English, I think, the "master", or perhaps "lord of the manor"? This is my home and you are welcome. You can call me -' he hesitated almost imperceptibly '- "Otxoa" - yes, that would be best.' He waved a hand in the direction of the open door. 'Please. Come inside. You are my guests.'

The warm wash of hospitality was somewhat spoiled by the scowling face of Wax Jacket and the way he jerked the stubby barrel of the Skorpion in the direction of the door. Almu and Joni had already gone inside and Guy and Camus followed suit.

They found themselves in a spacious and tastefully decorated hall. To the rear was a minstrels gallery and doors led off in three different directions. The floor was made of flagstones that looked like they had seen considerable use over the years, from both human feet and animal hooves. Along one of the long walls a fire burned in a modern looking grate and a desk stood nearby with a couple of comfortable chairs positioned in front.

Otoxa made his way to the high backed leather chair behind the desk and motioned for Guy to sit. He moved to do so and Camus followed.

The Frenchman's path was blocked by Wax Jacket, who stared him down then marched him out through one of the doors at the back of the hall. Almu took the second seat, with Guy's bag at her feet and Joni positioned himself out of Guy's line of sight just behind.

Guy held up his wrists, chafed by the plastic cable tie cuffs. His hands were swollen after so many hours of restraint.

'I've said it before and I'll say it again. Is this how you treat your guests?'

The man calling himself Otoxa was not to be thrown. His urbane manner did not falter for a moment. 'Some, yes. Those who deserve it. Guests are not always friends, Guy. But I would like to think that you are going to behave as my friend, so...'

He waved a hand in a cutting motion and Guy suddenly felt Joni's weight on his shoulder as he leaned over from behind. A sharp knife was in his hand, with a straight lambsfoot blade. One upward cut and Guy was free. He sat and rubbed his wrists, to ease the intense pins and needles sensation of being released after so long.

'And Camus? Is he part of the club too?'

A cloud passed over Otoxa's face for the first time.

'Leon Camus will never be a friend. He and his ugly little organisation have worked against our brothers over the border in France for centuries. He is simply the current leader of a group that have been a thorn in our sides all this time. His interests and ours are at odds with each other and so, therefore I find myself at odds with him. He will be…' - again he searched for the right word - 'detained until our little business here is satisfactorily concluded.'

'What is that business, Otxoa? Precisely?'

'Guy, I am a man of principle and honour. It is very simple. I give you my word that you will go on your way once you have handed over to me the media that you carry containing the list of names of all the French agents operating in and against Britain. That is the only thing you have that is of interest to me. Once it is mine, your freedom will be yours. It is that simple.'

'And if I choose not to comply?'

Otoxa looked pained and beside him, Almu shifted uncomfortably in her seat. 'Oh Guy, it is far better if you co-operate. If you do not, then Joni will simply have to persuade you to reconsider. There is nothing complicated about any of this. I simply need what you have. Please bear in mind that I do not also need you to live.'

Chapter 27

Leon Camus examined the walls of his prison with professional interest. The only light was provided by a single bulkhead lamp high on one wall. The switch was not in the room. The only furniture consisted of two small single beds and a bucket, the state of which both spoke to its intended purpose and the fact that it had been used for such in the past and simply emptied, rather than cleaned. The door was iron, heavy and outlined in rivets. It looked solid and old, though not quite as old as the rest of the building.

In one corner there was a small table with a pile of small bottles of water and some long-life chocolate filled croissants in individual foil wrappings. Camus wrinkled his nose in disgust more at those than at the bucket. The floor was packed earth but there was no joy there; he had already had a go at scraping at it and came to stone just a couple of centimetres down. There were no windows. The room itself was in a small outbuilding behind the main house in a second courtyard; as they walked through the low doorway Camus imagined it to have been cattle sheds or something similar originally.

He was thankful for the fact that Wax Jacket had cut off his bindings when he had shown him in, but he had nothing that he could do with his newly freed hands besides scratch and pick his nose.

He laid down gingerly on one of the uncomfortable cots to wait.

--o-0-o--

At the same time, Guy Miller stood just a short distance away in the inner courtyard of the baserri. He was completely naked.

Guy's conversation with Otxoa was short and, from the latter's point of view, fruitless.
It hadn't gone well for Guy either. At first he had fallen back on his Royal Navy and SBS training and simply refused to co-operate. His Billingham had been tipped out onto the desk in front of him along with the contents of his pockets - with some "encouragement" from Joni.

Almu had absented herself at that point, looking distressed. Rubbing the side that had received the kick from Camus in the Plaza followed now by a couple of encouraging rabbit punches from Joni, Guy had watched her go and with her any hope he might have had of leniency.

Otxoa stirred through his belongings with a letter opener in the shape of a dagger. For a mad moment Guy had tensed himself to grab it from him but he knew it would be futile. Joni was itching for an excuse to hit him again and Guy wanted to avoid that as long as he could; he was not young anymore and every blow took his breath away and took longer to recover from.

Otxoa went through everything from his pockets and bag with an attention to detail that bordered on the obsessive. He picked up Guy's wallet and emptied cards and cash onto the table.

A laminated, passport-sized photo of Jane had fluttered to the floor and Guy had bent forward to pick it up. Joni took the opportunity to kick him hard in the knee - his bad knee - and he had dropped hard to the floor with a low moan. Joni had picked him up and deposited him back into the chair then resumed his position just out of sight.

Otxoa had repeated the same two questions over and over.

"What is this?" and "Where is the micro SD card?" To the first, Guy would answer truthfully each time. "A lens. A spare battery. A credit card." To the latter he stuck to the same answer. "I do not understand the question." Sometimes Otxoa ignored his response and moved on. Sometimes he waved the letter opener at Guy, without looking up. Each time he did that, Joni slapped Guy in the head.

This went on until Otxoa had trawled through every item on the table. Sometimes he validated Guy's responses by Googling the item on a small MacBook on one side of his desk. When he was done he sat back in his chair and gently drew the sharp point of the letter opener down his cheek as he regarded Guy.

He had then instructed Guy to strip. Guy did so, stumbling a little as he tried to keep his balance on his bad leg while removing his trousers. Joni took each item of clothing as he took it off, feeling the pockets and the seams, and running a small metal detector over each item before throwing them in a corner in a heap.

Nothing.

Otxoa used an intercom on the table and spoke rapidly in a language that Guy could not understand. Wax Jacket had re-appeared almost immediately. Guy had then been dismissed with the ominous instruction to Joni - "Persuade him to co-operate." Joni had unholstered his pistol and taken him from the hall through the same door that Wax Jacket had taken Camus an hour or so before. Behind him, Otxoa had waved to Wax Jacket to clear his desk of Guy's belongings.

It was cold in the courtyard. The sun had gone down leaving only a faint glow in the Western sky. Guy could hear rooks cawing not far away, railing at the dying of the light. He stood in front of a muddy white wall, with an elderly Lada Niva parked a short distance away. It was clearly used for farm duties and had seen better days.

At that moment, Guy felt much the same. He hadn't volunteered for this. At all.

Bowman had painted a convivial picture of Wayfarers wafting their way around the globe in gentlemanly comfort, shuttling ultra top secret messages to and fro on behalf of The Crown. He hadn't mentioned the likelihood of being chased across Europe by a French fop or treated like a punchbag by nut-job nationalists.

In the palm of his hand he still held the photo of Jane he had retrieved from the floor in front of Otxoa's desk; they could take his clothes and his freedom but he would not let them take from him his primary reason for living.

The gloom was pierced by the glare of a couple of high-wattage spotlights. They illuminated where he was standing and threw the rest of the courtyard into darkness. 'Fuck you.' He said, and stood up straight, staring into the dark where he had last seen Joni standing, smoking a cigarette. As he squinted he fancied he could see the faint red glow of the tip.

It turned out that he was wrong, by about eight feet to the left. He learned of his error when a high pressure jet of water struck him in the groin and knocked him back against the wall with a bang. Winded and disorientated, Guy struggled to regain his feet but the hand directing the hose had other ideas.

His legs were blasted out from under him then the spray was directed straight at his face. He gasped for breath and instinctively curled into a foetal position. The water was ice cold and kicked up the mud as it played over him.

Within moments he was freezing, deafened, breathless and covered in muck.

The assault continued for what seemed like hours but was in reality only minutes. Then the jet ceased abruptly and a deafening silence fell.

Guy lay still, curled into a ball, fighting for breath and shivering. As the ringing in his ears subsided he fancied he could hear laughter. He was clearly the main entertainment. He felt rather than heard footsteps and opened his eyes to see a pair of legs and feet in front of him.

Joni.

'Where is the micro SD card?' His accent was much thicker than Almu's and almost impenetrable compared to Otxoa. Guy was slow to respond, and the impatient and savage kick to his head would have knocked him out had he not rolled away enough to take the brunt of it on his shoulder. He rolled on his back and spat dirt and water before answering.
'Up.

Your.

Arse.'

The feet receded and the hose was turned on once more.

--o-0-o--

Roger Bowman looked up as the door to his office opened. Andre Lucas stepped in and shut it quietly behind him.

'Don't bother to knock - oh, you didn't...' Bowman said sarcastically. They knew each other well enough for it to be meant as a joke but as he looked at Lucas' face he saw that he was not in the mood for levity. 'What's on your mind, Andre?' He waited while Lucas lowered his lean frame into a guest chair and gathered his thoughts. He took just a heartbeat too long about it for Bowman to be comfortable. He turned away from the laptop at the side of his desk and faced Lucas square on.

'Roger, we need to talk.' He took a deep breath and leaned forward in the chair 'I've come from Ruth Owen's bedside. She's currently under MoD police guard at Frimley Park in Surrey. She went to Guy Miller's home this morning with a gun; we believe that she intended harm to Jane Miller. We don't know exactly why – yet, although we do have a fair idea of her overall motivation.'

He paused for breath and Bowman jumped in. 'Jane Miller - is she unharmed? Safe?'

'Yes to both, Resourceful lady. I might go as far as to say "scary".' Lucas allowed himself a tight smile.

'She managed to shoot Owen in both feet with a 12-bore from short range.'

In response to Bowman's raised eyebrow he continued '...I don't think she'll be painting what's left of her toenails for a while.'

Bowman's turn to smile. 'I've not met Mrs. Miller but we have, ah, spoken. "Scary" is an apt word. And we don't know why?'

'No, but it's obviously something to do with Miller's current journey. I don't for a moment think she was operating alone. An IP check of her mobile showed that she had a second phone and that she has made and received a number of calls from a French mobile number in the past weeks. I also have a trace running on her financial affairs to see if there are any anomalies.'

'Phone records - is that how you got onto her?'

'Yes. And my investigations within the Wayfarers turned up something else as well.'

'Oh?' Bowman's attention had started to wander again as another email toast notification popped up in the corner of his laptop screen and caught his eye. He turned back to face Lucas.

'Roger. I know about you and Beth Shepherd.'

Silence.

'Please, do me the courtesy of not denying it.'

Bowman returned Lucas' steady gaze. 'I wouldn't be so uncouth. It's clear you've done your homework before this conversation.'

'Naturally.'

'What do you think you know, Andre?'

Lucas recounted the conversation with Shepherd. Bowman stared into space as he spoke and slowly lowered the lid on his laptop.

'It wasn't her fault.'

'True or not, I would have been disappointed had you not said that - and I am disappointed enough in you already.'

Bowman sighed. 'Andre, it happened. I'm not proud of it. Timing, and all that. Nobody was ever meant to get hurt, least of all Beth Shepherd.'

'Or Julia Bowman...? Or Iain, or Edith or Calum?'

Bowman straightened in his chair as if electrocuted.

'Don't bring my fucking FAMILY into this, Andre. You forget...'

'I forget nothing, Roger. Least of all the collateral damage you have caused by your infidelity. Do you expect to keep your job when this comes out? Or your *wife*?' Lucas shook his head. 'Your position is untenable. You are *compromised*. God, Roger, just how *stupid* are you?

Bowman sat for a long minute before answering. 'Scale of 1 to 10? Probably about 11. I report direct to Her Majesty the *Queen*, Andre. Given her own mucky family history, how do you think she is likely to react? Let alone Julia...' He paused and fixed Lucas with a penetrating stare. 'I know I shouldn't ask but, is there any way to...'

'No. And I really wish you hadn't. It doesn't help and I have now lost what shred of respect I still had for you.

It gets worse. Your little indiscretion appears to be common knowledge in the Wayfarers, Roger. In fact, I'd go further - I actually seem to be the very last to know. Ruth Owen knew. She told me. And even Danny Romano – one of the least observant men I have ever met. I asked him in the car on the way back from the hospital. There's no way out from this one. You will have to tender your resignation.'

Bowman sighed, nodded. 'Alright. You're right.

I know you are right. I shall. But I want to do one more thing on my watch. See Miller home safely. I sent him on this journey; I have to see it through. Will you let me do that?'

'It's not my choice, Roger. It's yours. But I will refrain from taking any further action for 24 hours - that should be long enough for him to get back. And then, when he touches British soil, you resign. Agreed?'

Bowman knew he had nowhere to go. 'Agreed.'

The knock at the door made both men start. Linda DiSanto stuck her head around.

'Sir - Sirs? Guy Miller's card has been used in Northern Spain; in a town called Zarauz. And it wasn't him.'

Chapter 28

Wax Jacket's real name was Eneko Azkuna. He had not been with Otxoa's operation for long. He was taken on because of his unquestioning willingness to do some of the jobs that others shied away from.

He was not afraid to get his hands messy, even if that mess was blood. He was a drinking buddy of Joni's, who had vouched for him and brought him into the fold. Drink was just a pastime to Joni but to Eneko it was a passion and it was slowly consuming him.

He could never get enough Damm, or enough money to pay for it. When he had cleared Otxoa's desktop of the Englishman's belongings he had palmed the credit card and it was now burning a hole in his pocket as he drove. He was not stupid enough to think that he could pass for Guy Miller, and he had no idea of the PIN number of the card, but it had the contactless symbol on the front and he knew that he could use it without challenge as long as he kept the value of any one transaction below 25 Euro.

At the end of his shift he had excused himself and headed home to the flat he shared with his elder brother and his young family on the outskirts of Zarautz. They had been born there, and had watched the town become more and more gentrified and they and their friends and family pushed further to the fringes of both the town and society.

His brother made a living dealing weed and Eneko was not averse to sampling his wares on a regular basis.

His brother had a small cannabis farm hidden in a barn in Argoin Auzoa and Eneko sometimes helped with the harvest in return for a few ounces for personal use. He lit up now and inhaled deeply as he sat in his battered Fiat across the street from an Eroski grocery shop. The brightly lit shop sold liquor as well as beer and he was mentally calculating how much rum and Damm he could buy for just under 25 Euro.

Five minutes later, he knew. Humming happily to himself he loaded his purchases into the back seat and set off for the next late-night Supermercado to try his luck again.

--o-0-o--

'Here.' Linda DiSanto tapped a well manicured nail on the monitor screen in front of her. Bowman and Lucas leaned closer with interest and studied the map on the screen.

'Za..ra..utz' Bowman pronounced carefully. 'Where's that?'

DiSanto zoomed the map out with a few mouse clicks. 'It's a resort town in Northern Spain - Basque country. Nice beaches - according to TripAdvisor.

Miller's credit card was used there a little over an hour ago. A contactless transaction in an Eroski supermarket on the outskirts of town. The purchase was beer and rum.'

'Miller might be thirsty...' Bowman said, testing the waters. Lucas snorted.

'He'd have to be very thirsty, Sir. There was an almost identical transaction at a nearby Carrefour about 15 minutes later, just as I was coming to fetch you.'

Lucas looked confused. 'How do we know about this so quickly? I mean, I know that we track a Wayfarer's chip and PIN card transactions as a matter of course, but isn't contactless mostly validated offline? It can take hours to get a transaction notified to the bank, can't it?

DiSanto allowed herself a small smile. This was her speciality. 'Yes Sir. Normally. But we struck lucky. The nightly batch synchronisation with the card provider took place almost at the same time, just a few minutes later. Once it tagged, I put on a trace for anything similar in the area - anything.'

Lucas looked impressed. 'I genuinely didn't know we could do that.' He said. 'Useful...'

DiSanto beamed. 'We couldn't until very recently, Sir. It's a spin-off from recent developments.

You've heard of "Weeping Angel"?' 'The British tech used by the CIA to spy on people with smartphones and Samsung tellys? - yes, of course.'

'Well, it's sort of similar. We took the basic Weeping Angel functionality and allied it with some of our existing bulk analytics capabilities to create proxy avatars that proactively stalk the internet sniffing for specific trigger events. It even sits behind our keyword listening these days; much less labour-intensive and we no longer have to sub-contract to GCHQ.' She sat back and folded her arms 'We can actually know more about specific bank transactions than the banks themselves.'

'That wouldn't be hard' Lucas snorted. He turned to Bowman 'Why wasn't I aware of this?' Bowman dismissed him with the palm of his hand. 'Above your pay grade, Andre.' He turned his attention back to DiSanto.

'What can we actually do with this information? Can we find out who is using Miller's card, for a start?'

'Not retrospectively, Sir, without somebody on the ground to actually go to the shops and see if they can lay hands on any security tapes. There's nothing I can find or hack into online so I assume both outlets are low-tech and just have local closed loop video, if anything at all. I'm sorry...'

'Don't be. You've given us a place to start.'

Bowman turned to Lucas.

'Andre, I have a bad feeling about this. Miller's on his very first journey for the Wayfarers and we already know that he has Camus and the bloody DGER hard on his arse. If something's happened and he's in trouble we need to locate him and...'

'"Extract with vigour". Yes, I know.'
Lucas tapped the blue area of the map on-screen with his index finger. 'Bay of Biscay. Are there any usable assets in the area?'

DiSanto called across to a colleague a couple of stations away. 'Ilan, can you check the Admiralty data feed and see if there are any ships in or near the Bay of Biscay with a heli capability?' The answer was short in coming, as Ilan's fingers darted across the keys.

'RFA *Wave Ruler* is traversing the Bay of Biscay at the moment. She's been on FOST support for the past few months and is now heading to the Gulf to support Royal Navy operations there. She's a Fast Fleet Tanker with...' Ilan checked his screen for more detail and continued '...a civilian crew of 80-odd and a small number of Royal Navy personnel aboard at all times. She has one Merlin heli of her own and...' He flipped a screen and allowed himself a small smile as he checked the manifest 'a company of Royal Marines hitching a ride to Oman.'

Lucas nodded. 'Thanks Ilan.' After a moment's thought he continued 'Please make to Duty Fleet Commander, Operations, Northwood from Wayfarer Shepherd One: "Request immediate logistical support of RFA Wave Ruler currently in sea area Biscay for urgent stress urgent Wayfarer Red Op. Dayword is "remedy", authority Lucas One-Seven-Two-Five-Alpha. Confirm and co-ordinate. Wayfarer assets inbound by heli, imminent, details follow."' He paused for breath then continued.

'Let me know the response. Then get me a flight quick as you can from Northolt down to RNAS Yeovilton - four pax.' He turned to face Bowman. 'All things being equal my team and I will get there within a few hours, Roger. Yeovilton has Merlins ready to generate at all times. I should be able to organise a lift to *Wave Ruler* through the CO there, Commodore Mark Kimber - if you can you smooth the way…'

'Yes, I know what to do with the MoD. They'll moan but they'll co-operate.

They're already asking me what I want done with Detective Sergeant Owen. Once we have a sniff at a precise location for Miller, Andre, you will be the first to know.' He put a hand on Lucas' shoulder. Their earlier animosity was on hold; there was a job to do.

'Bring him home, Andre. Bring him home.'

--o-0-o--

Leon Camus awoke as the sound of bolts being drawn back on the iron door echoed through the small cell. As he sat up the door opened and Guy Miller was thrown into the room. He landed hard and fetched up against the cot opposite his own. He was aghast at the state of the Englishman.

He was filthy, caked in mud and dried blood and completely naked. He lay still where he fell. Camus ripped the blanket from his own bed and wrapped it around Miller's shoulders as he helped him to sit on the cot. Behind him the door slammed shut and they were alone.

Guy shivered uncontrollably and hugged the blanket tight around his shoulders. Camus fetched one of the water bottles from the table, cracked the seal and pulled out the nozzle before offering it to Guy. Guy focussed on it with bleary eyes then waved it away. He started to speak, but choked. He reached up and pulled something from his mouth. Camus only caught a glimpse, but it looked like a laminated photo of a smiling woman.

'I've swallowed enough water to drown twice. I don't need you to help me on my way.'

Camus sat on the cot opposite, facing Guy.

He clasped his hands together around his knees and spoke.

'Guy, *mon ami*, what have they done to you?' He regarded the Englishman with a sympathetic eye. 'No clothes, the mud, the blood - is it yours? And what on earth is that on your toe?'

Guy smiled for the first time in what felt like days. 'Yes, the blood is mine. I haven't quite worked out where from yet.' He held up his foot. 'This - is a Compeed blister plaster. They stick like limpets if you put them on according to the instructions.' He shrugged. 'Looks like I can still do something right.'

Camus looked critical. He crossed again to the table and brought back a couple of the long-life croissants. He handed one to Guy and unwrapped his own, then swapped them over when he realised Guy was in no state to fiddle with the wrapping. He opened the second, took a bite, pulled a face and wrapped it again before putting it on the cot at his side.

'Guy, I will not lie to you. This does not look good. Why not give these men what they want? Do you really want to die for your country? It is a rather outmoded concept, no?'

'You've changed your tune. It wasn't long ago that you were trying hard to kill me.'

'That was different. I was working for the honour of France. England has no honour to defend; she puts her soldiers in harm's way and does not stop them being sued years later by those who were trying very hard to kill them. Your Prime Minister is a woman and your Foreign Minister a buffoon. Are these the people you want to die for?'

'Not for them, no. But I have a task to complete, and I will do it to the best of my ability, regardless of you or a bunch of Spanish thugs getting in my way. Call it a habit.'

Camus shrugged. 'Have it your way.' Personally I think that you are a misguided fool.'

Guy started to respond but at that moment the single bulkhead light snapped off, throwing them into darkness.

'It seems that they want us rested, at least.' Camus said with a sigh. He stripped the blanket from his own filthy mattress and tossed it over to Guy in the darkness. 'Here. Your need is greater than mine, I think. *Bonne nuit*, Guy.'

Guy caught the blanket and used it to wrap himself further. The shivering had at least subsided and he was exhausted. He finished the croissant, barely tasting it, and laid back on the cot. In his left hand he held the small photo of Jane.

He had nearly lost his grip on it in the battering from the hose, but in a moment of desperation had put it in his mouth and held it in one cheek, like a hamster.

Right now he felt it was his only link to his normal life - and thinking of Jane was the only thing keeping him going right now. He lay in the darkness and stared up at where the ceiling must be, his mind in turmoil. Deep down he didn't think that he could take much more of the treatment he had received at the hands of Joni. He was no spy; he had no means to resist interrogation beside the techniques taught by the Royal Navy and SBS, and that was decades ago, now and a hell of a lot easier if you were fitter and younger.

He felt every one of his years at that point; there was very little of him that did not ache right now. Beside him Camus seemed to have no trouble sleeping, at least judging by the deep, heavy breathing that had started almost immediately the Frenchman had stopped talking. Guy was certain that he would not be able to sleep himself.

That was his last thought as he dozed off.

Chapter 29

It had been a hectic few hours for Lucas and his team. The flight from Northolt to Somerset in an RAF BAe 146 had been smooth, swift and uneventful; the landing at the busiest military airfield in the Westcountry was somewhat less so.

RNAS Yeovilton is the home of a number of Fleet Air Arm and RAF squadrons, mostly operating helicopters. For Lucas and his team it was a logical staging point; the nearest landing place sufficiently close to the main Royal Marine Commando base in Devonport capable of taking the 146.

Their flight plan, however, was not part of routine operations for the day and their pilot - a seasoned Flight Lieutenant - had only been cleared for final approach a few short minutes ago. Bowman pulling strings back in London again.

The landing lights at the big airfield had come into view and the RAF pilot - a veteran of flights under combat conditions into and out of Kabul and other hostile places - had angled the agile 146 into a steep approach before slamming the landing gear hard onto the runway.

They were strained against their four-point safety harnesses by his sharp braking manoeuvre, using full flaps and reverse thrust as he brought the aircraft to a quick stop then taxied to the terminal building.

They had been met by an irritated looking Marines Lieutenant who had motioned them to follow him to a couple of dark blue Defenders parked in a "no waiting" zone at the front of the building. There was nobody there who seemed interested in moving them on - a far cry, Lucas thought ruefully, to somewhere like Heathrow.

They were whisked at speed across the airbase in a tight convoy and waved through the gates of the Royal Marines facility with the minimum of delay to check identification. There was no ceremony; Lucas, Romano, Barratt and Shepherd were shown straight to a briefing room and issued with immersion suits then sat in front of a short safety video on the Merlin 3.

As the video ended the lights went up and the Lieutenant who had collected them from the 146 reappeared, following close behind a ramrod straight man in his mid forties who wore on the shoulders of his shirt the two pips and crown of a full Colonel in the Royal Marines. He in turn was followed by a hard-faced man in an immersion suit topped somewhat incongruously by a green beret. The latter positioned himself by the door "at ease" and stared pointedly into the middle distance.

'Langley.' The senior officer said as his eyes scanned the group and settled on Lucas, standing still by the window. 'Are you OC?'

'Andre Lucas, Queens Wayfarers. This is my team.' He named each in turn, nodding at them as he did so.

"We need a lift, Sir, to RFA *Wave Ruler*. I'd like to borrow one of your Merlins so that…"

Colonel Langley held up a hand. 'I'm aware of your "needs", *Mr.* Lucas although I confess I was unaware of your… unit - until informed by Commodore Kimber. It seems that your very existence is strictly "need to know" - and until half a bloody hour ago I didn't.'

Lucas made to respond but the Colonel's hand raised once more. 'Mr. Lucas, I don't want to hear it and I have not finished. Your unscheduled arrival has titted about in a very big way with my ops. schedules not to mention necessitating my releasing - under protest - a Merlin Mk. 3 of 846 Naval Air Squadron to act as your personal taxi for the day.' He stopped and took a deep breath, then jerked a thumb at the silent soldier by the door. 'This is Colour Sergeant Hood, one of my best men.

He will be your …liaison. His brief is to facilitate your *jaunt* and ensure that we get our heli back in one piece. He will co-ordinate with the Marine Commando detachment already on board *Wave Ruler* and make sure that you don't get thrown straight overboard on arrival.'

He paused again, then continued in a low voice. 'He also has my personal orders to keep a bloody close eye on you and your crew.

One step out of line, Lucas, just one, and I will have your arse on a silver platter and no amount of friends in high places will stop me. Clear?'

Lucas looked hard at Langley. He came across like another Lefevre, but there was a crucial difference - there was another way to deal with him. He straightened as he turned to Hood and snapped off a crisp salute. 'Colours. It's a pleasure to have you with us.' The Colour Sergeant returned the salute almost on a reflex and a moment of uncertainty clouded his face. Neither he nor his Colonel were aware of Lucas' own background and they had judged him, as many did, by his somewhat scruffy outward appearance. Out of the corner of his eye Lucas noticed Romano stifle a smirk and he shot him a furious glare before turning his attention back to Colonel Langley.

'We are grateful, Sir. It will be a huge help to get us there as quickly as possible.'

Langley nodded, then relaxed slightly and leaned closer in a conspiratorial manner. 'Lucas - or whatever your name is - what's the urgency? I've never known such a flap for four civilians, let alone the whole damn base being turned upside down to scramble a heli for anything less than a terrorist strike.' He raised an eyebrow. "Hmm...?"

Lucas looked pensive for a moment before responding.

'It's really best that you know as little as possible, Colonel. Deniability and all that. As to why; suffice to say that there is an ex-Royal Navy officer in distress somewhere in Spain and it's our job to sort things out. Rest assured we'll look after your heli, and your Colour Sergeant, come to that. Our job is to get people back in one piece.'

Langley and Hood exchanged glances then Langley spoke. 'Why didn't you say so before? Stop hanging about and get airborne.'

He paused then snapped a salute of his own at Lucas before turning on his heel and departing, followed by his aide.

The door shut behind them leaving Hood alone with Lucas and his team. He spoke for the first time.

'You lot had better get a move on. Putting on one of these suits if you've not done it before is like trying to fit a condom to a randy tomcat. We'll be wheels-up in 15 minutes and you won't be allowed on if you aren't properly suited and booted.'

Lucas allowed himself a wry smile as he looked around at his team. 'We'll manage, Colours. We always do.'

Chapter 30

Camus sat up, blinking and rubbing his eyes as the bulkhead light snapped on and the unmistakable sound of a key in a lock echoed through the small cell he shared with Guy Miller. Guy stirred, but remained inside the blanket in which he had spent the night cocooned. The door opened and Almu stepped gingerly inside. She carried a pile of clothes, which she laid on the end of Guy's cot. Behind her the door was closed and re-locked.

Almu stood uncertainly. She looked at Guy's blanket-wrapped form then at Camus, who shrugged.

'What do you expect, *ma petite*? Your English friend has had a hard time, thanks to you.' Camus stood and stretched then walked to the table, helping himself to another water bottle.

'She's no friend of mine. She can fuck right off.' Guy's voice was croaky, but he was clearly feeling more like himself after a night's sleep, even in such uncomfortable surroundings. He sat up and glared at Almu. 'What do you want?'

She looked at her boots for a moment then met his gaze. 'Guy, I am sorry. I really didn't think it would come to this. I did not think you would be so - so stubborn. Why can you not just give Otxoa what he wants?'

Guy fixed Almu with a steady glare. 'What's this, good cop, bad cop? Have you come here to soften me up before the next shower? Get out, Almu. You and your little playmates disgust me.'

'Guy, I understand why you say such a thing. I am sorry - truly sorry. But I do not want to see you hurt any further. I have brought you clothes because Otxoa will send for you shortly. He will not stop, Guy, until you give him the card.'

She took a deep breath. 'There is something you need to understand. Otxoa is *not* really ETA. Not any more. Our elected leaders – ETA's ruling council - have renounced violence and disarmed. They seek a peaceful settlement with the Spanish government now. Otxoa disagrees, fundamentally.

They disowned him for his extreme views. He has vowed to continue the fight in his own way. He and his small band of followers believe that the only way to win true independence for our people is via the gun and the bomb, both here and acoss the border in France. He has been disowned by the ETA Executive. Guy, he wants the information he knows you carry to sell to the highest bidder, to fund the purchase of new weapons. He won't just offer it to your British government but to anyone with enough money. He will stop at nothing to get it.' She paused, took a deep breath. 'Guy - you do not deserve to die.'

Camus cleared his throat.

'My dear, I have a question. I think it is relevant... If you have not the stomach for the fight, why are you associating with these thugs?'

Guy shot a glance at Camus and nodded. 'That's a good question. What *is* your motivation?'

Almu took time in replying. 'I report to the ETA Executive. My role is to keep watch on Otxoa and to report back on his activities. He is a threat to the peace process. Guy, you must believe me, I never thought all this would go so far, so fast. The things I have done I did to keep Otxoa's trust, no more. I have been trying to get a message out to my handler but I have no mobile signal here and no access to a landline. If I could stop all this I would. All I can do now is beg you to give him what he wants so that you do not die at my cousin's hand.'

Guy was about to respond when the door opened again. Joni's bulk filled the doorway. He stepped into the room and his place was taken by Wax Jacket, with his Skorpion at the ready. Joni jerked with a thumb and Almu left, but not before shooting a glance back at Guy. She mouthed one word - "please" - as she headed to the door. Wax Jacket grinned and turned only slightly sideways, forcing Almu to squeeze past him as best she could.

Joni pointed at the pile of clothes she had left at the end of the bed.
'Put them on. Now.'

'If you insist. I would normally shower first, but under the circumstances...'

Joni responded by pulling his Beretta from a shoulder holster and thumbing off the safety, before pointing it first at Guy then at Camus. The threat couldn't be clearer.

'Now.'

Guy did as he was told. The pile consisted of a set of greasy blue overalls and a pair of wellington boots. The boots were too large and the overalls too small. Guy realised that if he bent over he was likely to do himself some harm. He fastened the poppers as best he could.

As he stood he reached one hand under the blanket on the bed and palmed the small photo of Jane, slipping it into one of the pockets of the overalls. He followed Joni back along the corridors to the hall in which he first met Otxoa.

As they entered, he was standing with his back to a fire flickering warmly in the grate. He had changed from yesterday's casual country clothes to a sharp dark blue suit. A tie in the same colour stood out against a snow white shirt with a spread collar. His hair was neatly slicked back and even from some distance away he smelled good. Vetiver, thought Guy – the man at least had taste.

He looked for all the world like a wealthy Spanish businessman; a look completed by the file he held in his hands and seemed to be studying as they entered. He glanced up at their approach and motioned that Guy should be sat in the same chair as the day before.

'Guy, I trust you slept well? I am sorry if your accommodation is a little basic. Tell me, have you had time to consider my entirely reasonable request?'

Guy shrugged. 'Your facilities leave a lot to be desired. I wouldn't open this place as a bed and breakfast any time soon; you'll be torn apart on Tripadvisor.'

Otxoa ignored the jibe, choosing instead to walk back over to the table that contained Guy's belongings. He rifled through them once more until he came to the X-Pro2. He picked it up and peered through the viewfinder, pointing the camera at the fire and into the corners of the room before coming back to stand in front of Guy.

'You are a photographer, yes? It is your - pastime?'

'And my living. That's a tool of my trade. Please don't drop it. I'm not sure if my insurance covers damage by clumsy terrorist.'

Otxoa smiled. 'Guy, I am not a terrorist. I am a patriot.'

'From where I'm sitting you are a complete fruit-loop.'

Otxoa ignored him again, preferring instead to concentrate on the camera. He pointed at the top plate. 'Is this where you turn it on? I think I should take a photo of you. It will be the last photo of you alive. A nice memento for your dear wife, yes?'

Otxoa's right index finger turned the collar around the shutter release and in the quiet room Guy heard the faint electronic snicker as the Fuji came to life. He palmed the lens cap and pointed the 35mm lens at Guy's bruised face.

'I think you English always say "cheese" when someone takes your picture?'

'You're a bit out of date. We find we get a much better result by saying "threnodygild".'

--o-0-o--

Bowman sat alone in the Queen's Wayfarers meeting room, watching the globe silently rotate. He traced the letter inlaid on the wood in front of him with his fingertip, back and forth, over and over again. A cup of tea sat cold at his elbow. Since Lucas and his team had scrambled down to the Westcountry they had heard nothing further. No more hits on Miller's card, no hint of his own location.

He kept going over and over in his head the possibilities and options. Lucas could do nothing without a direction and a destination. Putting him and his team on board the *Wave Ruler* was an expedient move, given what they knew, but as an option it had a shelf-life.

Never mind the political shitstorm that would result if a Fleet Air Arm helicopter were to head without a flightplan straight into the airspace of a sovereign nation already touchy due to their ongoing dispute over the status of the Rock of Gibraltar; the diplomats could deal with that – shit happened.

Far more of a practical issue was that the RFA tanker was on a mission of it's own and even Bowman with all his political clout struggled to delay, let alone divert a Royal Fleet Auxiliary ship intent on Royal Navy business without a damn good reason.

The net result was that Lucas' Merlin, travelling at it's top speed of 167 knots would intercept the *Wave Ruler* in a little under an hour but the ship would continue it's course. It was following a fuel-efficient straight line in the sea lane across the top of the Bay of Biscay which meant that, when distance and fuel capacity were taken into consideration, there was only a window of opportunity of about five hours during which they were in range and able to interdict - depending of course where exactly in Spain they needed to get to.

Bowman sat back in his chair and rubbed his temples for the dozenth time. He had sat in the same seat in that room for years now and he had never known a journey get so messy so quickly. If nothing else it underscored the importance of the Wayfarer's very existence; the world was rapidly unravelling to become a very nasty place indeed and their innate ability to pass un-noticed and thus unmolested was a strategic asset.

Except in this instance, Miller's passing might just as well have been heralded in the Court Circular - or on Twitter. He stared at the globe and indulged in a spot of self-flagellation; the Wayfarers had become sloppy under his command; they had managed to operate largely un-noticed by history for hundreds of years, apart from a few scrapes here and there. There had been nothing untoward involving them in the Iberian Peninsula since the Napoleonic Wars - and now this. Owen's motivations were not fully understood but her intent had been clear. Damage to the realm.

He looked down at his mobile phone on the table beside his mug. He winced slightly. He had already deleted all Beth's texts - but that couldn't erase the damage that had been done. He also knew that he should call Jane Miller but he really didn't know what to say; at this stage, there was little he could.

He stared at the globe again. His letter of resignation was already written, sitting in the top drawer of his desk. Once Miller was feet-dry he would execute the contents and walk away - away from his life's work.

He deserved no less. No fool like an old fool, as his wife would no doubt say if she ever found out - something he still wanted to avoid at all costs - or did he? He came to a decision at that point. He would come clean - he could not live a lie. He would tell his wife the truth and suffer the consequences.

Strangely having come to that decision Bowman felt re-energised, as if a weight had been lifted. He stood and headed for the door of the Wayfarer's Ops. room, which opened as he approached.

Linda DiSanto beckoned him impatiently back into the dimly lit hub of Wayfarer activity. Bowman squared his shoulders, gathered his tea mug and headed in her direction. He had barely taken a step before she spoke.

'Sir. Miller's camera has just been activated within range of a wifi router.'

Chapter 31

Shepherd swallowed hard, making a valiant effort to hold on to her stomach as they lowered on to the pitching deck. The flight from Yeovilton to RFA *Wave Ruler* had been quite an experience. She'd flown in helis before of course, but the Merlin Mk3 was, in spite of it's modern specification, by far the most functional; there were no comforts at all. She was sitting in a canvas bucket seat in the cargo hold along the port side, with Romano and Barratt. Facing them opposite sat Lucas and Colour Sergeant Hood.

The latter had spent the flight from Yeovilton chewing rhythmically on a wad of gum, looking for all the world like a belligerent bull. His attention was focussed upon a spot on the far bulkhead when Lucas tapped him on the arm and indicated that he should switch channel to 4 for a private conversation. He did so and Lucas' voice sounded loudly in his headset.

'Colours. A question if I may. I heard and understood what Langley said but why are *you* here? A Colour Sergeant doesn't usually liaise – or nursemaid. He could have put a lower rank on this. What's your story?'

Hood sat silent, immobile. Lucas started to think that he had not heard, then the Commando spoke.

'I'm nearing the end of my time in the corps. I'll be a civilian in two months. I'm looking for a billet and when I heard about this jaunt of yours I volunteered to tag along. I don't know if you have any jobs going, but I do know that this looks more interesting than signing on.'

Lucas stretched out one of his cramped legs and shifted in his seat before replying. 'I'll be blunt. I'm not recruiting right this moment, but I may have a vacancy shortly.' His eyes flicked for an instant over at where Shepherd sat clenching her jaw and trying not to throw up.

'There are a number of hoops you would need to pass through, but when we are back in the UK I'll give you my details, okay? For now I just want to focus on the job in hand.'

'Understood and agreed, Sir.'

They rendezvoused with the *Wave Ruler* 55 minutes later and the Fleet Air Arm pilot performed a textbook landing. The three Rolls Royce Turbomeca engines died to a low grumble as crewmembers bustled about, securing them to the deck.

They had been taken below immediately and led to yet another of the briefing rooms that seemed to abound in the armed forces, either on land or sea. This one, however, had the advantage of large mugs of steaming hot tea and well-stuffed bacon rolls.

Lucas and his team had not held back - it had been a long time since their last meal in London. Even Shepherd tucked in, to, as she said, steady her stomach. Hood disappeared as soon as they arrived, having been intercepted on the way below deck by a Royal Marines Corporal.

No sooner had they sat down than Lucas was himself collected by a naval rating who led him to the ship's Comms. Office. He was greeted by the Officer of the Watch, a young Lieutenant named Bailey, who directed him to sit at one of the vacant consoles and don a headset. Bailey then turned and asked the two technicians working at other consoles to step out for a few minutes, before leaving himself.

Within moments a familiar voice spoke, sounding slightly hollow in the noise cancelling headphones.

'Andre? It's Roger.'
'Roger. Have you news?'

'Yes. We have a location for Miller. His camera was switched on fifteen minutes ago. Andre, he gave the word almost immediately.'
Lucas' face tautened and he leaned forward involuntarily.

'Where is he, Roger? What's his status? Are we headed to Zarautz?'

'No. He's not there. But he is in Northern Spain. The router his camera connected to has been backtracked to a remote farmhouse on the coast just outside a town called Getaria; it's called Baserri Otxoa. I've shared the co-ordinates with Lieutenant Bailey there, and he is passing them to your pilot as we speak. Andre, we couldn't make out much of what was being said but from what we could hear - briefly - he was being interrogated for the dispatch. I think time is of the essence on this one, Andre. You need to go and get him.'

'We're on our way.' He turned to the Lieutenant who held out a sheaf of papers to him just as Bowman continued. 'We've sent through as much info as we could gather. The building is substantial; he could be anywhere inside and we have no idea of how many people are there, any alarms - or defences.'

Lucas nodded as he looked through the PDFs and photos then realised that Bowman couldn't see him. 'We will proceed with caution. We also appear to have acquired a useful asset - he's called Hood.'

Minutes later the Merlin was in the air again, headed straight for the Spanish coast. Lucas and his team were on board along with CSgt Hood but they had company now; three more Royal Marines in full combat gear had been co-opted by Hood from the complement already on Wave Ruler. "Insurance", he called it.

They sat along the sides of the helicopter in focused silence and between them all on a rapid deployment ramp most of the room in the loading bay was now taken up by a small Rigid Raider. This boat was to be their route to shore; more of Hood's doing. Lucas stole a glance at the Colour Sergeant, sitting impassive as before, chewing his gum. The man had a useful knack for getting things done.

In the cockpit, Flight Lieutenant David Booker thumbed the transmit button and established contact with the Spanish *Salvamento Maritimo*, or coast guard. In clipped tones he declared a navigational emergency while on a training flight and requested that any available units of the *Servicio Maritimo de la Guardia Civil* should stand by to assist in case their situation deteriorated.

They bore on towards the Spanish coast and he gradually lost height. He nodded across to Petty Officer Phil Owen, his loadmaster for the past 18 months and watched as the latter thumbed the intercom button.

'Stand by, Stand by. Drop in three minutes on my mark.'

Booker demonstrated his skills once more as he held the Merlin rock steady inches above the waves.

Hood and the Royal Marines in the loading bay sprang into action and within a couple of minutes the sleek dark shape of the Royal Marines Rigid Raider was arrowing across the water, heading for a landfall just to the east of Getaria as the Merlin clawed back into the sky and Booker declared their emergency over. Lucas checked his watch; nearly two hours since the camera had been activated. He could only hope that Miller was holding up.

--o-0-o--

Almu sat in the spacious kitchen with her head in her hands. Even through the heavy oak door she could hear the sound of raised voices and the occasional soft thud. She bit her lip until she drew blood. Joni was her cousin, but right now she felt that she didn't know him at all.

It had been him who had got involved with Otxoa and his personal offshoot of ETA and she had followed along not just, as she had told Miller and Camus, to keep an eye on the leader, but also to try to keep her own cousin from getting himself in over his head. She realised with a sinking feeling that it was far too late for that now.

She glanced over her shoulder; there was no privacy in the farmhouse. The large, communal open areas were constantly occupied with people, on both legitimate and clandestine business. She looked for the hundredth time at the screen of her phone - not a single bar.

The thick walls of the farmhouse combined with it's remote location meant that she couldn't get a mobile signal to save her life - or, she feared, Miller's.

She stood as the voices suddenly got louder - the door had been opened and Joni stepped through. He crossed to the sink and ran his right hand under the cold tap; his knuckles were bruised from the beating he had just administered. Almu fought back tears and tried not to run as she went back into Otxoa's spacious hall.

Guy was upright, at least. He sat in the chair with a towel held to his face to staunch the flow of blood from his right nostril. Otxoa had exited through another door and Guy was currently being guarded by Eneko Azkuna. As she strode across the flagstone floor she saw him take a malicious swipe at Guy, who at least still had the presence of mind to roll with the blow, lessening it's impact.

'Stop!' She shouted. 'It is *not* your place to do that.' Azkuna started guiltily then resumed his composure and grinned at her. She didn't know him well, and she didn't want to - but she knew his type. A large, sly ego compensated for a small brain and a mean soul. She crossed the room in a few long strides and stood by Guy, examining his face. Joni had been selective; most of the damage was superficial, but it would hurt like hell.

'Guy, why will you not tell him? This can only end one way.'

Guy smiled at her and winced as the action split his lip again. He dabbed at the fresh red blood with the towel and shook his head.

'Just too stupid, I suppose.'

'Your English friend is a man of courage and principle.
I admire that.'

Almu whirled. Otxoa had returned. His suit and shirt still looked immaculate but his tie was loosened. He was drying his hands with a towel similar to the one held by Guy. He was not the type to get his hands bloody directly but he found it tiring to watch so much physical violence.

'I have just been explaining to Guy that time is running short. I have a number of - associates - coming tonight. They expect me to have the information he carries and one of them – the one who names the highest price - will reward me handsomely for making it available to them.' He walked back to stand in front of Guy and prodded him repeatedly in the forehead. 'If. I. Do. Not. Get. It. I. Will. Not. Be. Happy. And you, Guy - you will not be alive.'

Joni rejoined them at that moment. Otxoa looked from him to Guy, and back again. 'Your water games last night did not have the desired effect and it seems that Mr. Miller is too dim to respond to a good beating. What do you intend now?'

Joni smiled. 'More water.' He said with a wolfish grin. 'There is a well in the courtyard...'

Chapter 32

Lucas and Hood stood side by side in a thicket of trees on a hillside overlooking Baserri Otxoa. Lucas handed back the Colour Sergeant's binoculars and stared down into the main courtyard.

'I make it the thick end of a dozen men. Some appear to be armed, but I wouldn't mind betting there's more weaponry lying around inside that place for the others if they feel the need to repel unwelcome visitors.' Hood nodded and pointed at the gates.

'Two ways in, only one big enough to take a large vehicle. The other is at the back and appears to lead into a kitchen. Two courtyards, one large, at the front and one small at the back. The smaller of the two appears to be used as a utility area; the larger is where they park their cars.' He nodded to a shadowy shape in the distance, climbing down from a telegraph pole; one of the Royal Marine Commando detachment from *Wave Ruler*, now under Hood's command.

'We're routed into their comms and can sever them at will, including jamming any mobile signals. There's nothing Earth-shattering going through except that they seem to be getting ready for some sort of visit later on. There have been a couple of international calls on the landline. There's also some encrypted data traffic - we don't have the kit with us to crack that. No mention at all of your boy, and no sign of him - not that I would expect them to be parading him in public, even given the remoteness of the location.'

Lucas' earpiece clicked twice and he thumbed the comms button on his chest. It was Romano.

'We've liberated a truck, Sir, from another farm a couple of K away. It's a Mercedes Unimog. Not pretty but it is heavy. We're heading back in your direction.'

Lucas acknowledged and turned back to Hood. 'Romano and Shepherd have got us some wheels, Colours. All we need to do is decide how best to use it.' the Commando nodded and checked his watch.

'Two of my men are around the back now. They are carrying shaped charges. We can use them to distract - or to secure access. They will plant the charges then hold position awaiting instructions.' Lucas nodded then pressed his comms button once more.

'Barratt - are you there?'

--o-0-o--

It would be fair to say that Peter Barratt hadn't been recruited by Andre Lucas into the Wayfarers for his personality or ready wit, or indeed for his flexibility in thought or deed. In fact, much like the rifle whose sights he was zeroing as he acknowledged Lucas' call, he was something of a specialist asset. In the right hands the Barrett Model 107A1 sniper rifle can hurl a .50 calibre shell over 1500 yards with startling accuracy and deadly results.

Barratt, the man, was Lucas' insurance policy. His sole role in an extraction operation was to position himself at a distance somewhere that gave him an overview of the primary location and to act - if necessary, and called upon to do so by Lucas - as an option of last resort. He had only had to go kinetic once, in Naples in 2015 - but he had performed then with surgical accuracy. Now, he had positioned himself in the bough of a tree such that he had an excellent view into both courtyards. He checked his harness once more, shifted his weight on his padded mat and lay in wait. When his earpiece crackled he assured Lucas that he was more than ready.

--o-0-o--

Guy Miller found himself back in the same small courtyard as the night before. This time it was daylight; he looked around at where he had been doused by the high pressure hose a few hours before and shivered involuntarily. He watched as Joni and another armed man hauled a metal cover off a low brick built well in one corner.

It fell to the ground with a clatter. At one time it was probably the primary source of fresh water for the Baserri, but no more; a foul stench of stagnant water and decay wafted across to where Guy stood. He shifted his weight uncomfortably and was rewarded with a sharp poke in the ribs from Wax Jacket. Almu stood off to one side, beside Otxoa who had decided this time to witness events himself.

Joni had hung back for a minute but appeared with Leon Camus and a length of rope. Camus was already restrained - cable tie cuffs were back on his wrists, behind his back. As Guy looked on, Joni abruptly kicked his legs out from under him and, with the help of a couple of other men, held him down while he passed a couple of loops of the rope around his ankles and back between his legs. He said something to the two men who had helped him and walked towards Guy as they laughed and dragged Camus unsteadily back to his feet. They held him firmly by an arm each. Camus breathed heavily and swore creatively at the men holding him.

As Joni walked, he carefully paid the rope out behind him. When he reached where Guy was standing, he handed him what was left, a coil about ten feet long. He turned back to the men restraining Camus and barked an order.

Guy looked on in horror as he suddenly realised what was about to happen, quickly wrapped a couple of loops of the rope around his body and braced himself as best he could. From what sounded like a mile away he heard Almu scream "NO!" as Camus was lifted bodily and hurled head-first down the well.

A split second later the Frenchman's full weight hit Guy's already exhausted body. He scrabbled across the dirt floor and overbalanced as Camus dropped like a stone. His terrified scream was cut short as he hit the water at the bottom with an oily splash.

Guy lay thunderstruck for a moment then jumped back to his feet and started to haul grimly on the rope in a grim parody of a tug of war. At first he made no headway, then gradually he started to regain ground. One step then another, then a few yards in front of - and below - him he was rewarded with the sound of spluttering, coughing and swearing.

He put his back into it but realised that he just about raise Camus higher in the well; he could not actually pull him out without help. He gritted his teeth and dug in his heels; his knee gave way for a moment and he slipped back another foot. The terrified cry from the well was heartbreaking and he redoubled his efforts, ignoring as best he could the pain that was threatening to engulf him.

Otxoa swam into his field of view and bent down close to Guy's sweating face.

'Give me the Micro SD card, Guy and all this will be over; we will haul the Frenchman up. You will not have his death on your conscience today - you have my word.' He straightened, and continued. 'But, if you do not - you will have to live with the consequences of your - stubbornness - for the rest of your life.'

Guy hauled on the rope and stood his ground. It started to cut into his shoulder and he despaired of ever getting out of this situation alive - let alone Camus.

He had no love for the French operative – In the past couple of days he had held him at knife and gunpoint and tried to kill him more than once - but he could not countenance himself being responsible for the man's death.

Otxoa walked along the line of the taut rope and ran a finger delicately along it, as if looking for dust. He tutted as he examined his fingertip and wiped it with a handkerchief he pulled from his suit breast pocket. "What do you say, Guy? Does the Frenchman live - or die? It is strictly your choice now."

Guy made to respond but bile filled his mouth and he could not. He knew he could not hold on much longer. Otxoa was right – no matter what, he could not let Camus die. The game was over. He had lost.

The dull crump of the three explosions, so close together as to be almost one, barely registered on his consciousness. A thick cloud of smoke and dust rose from the far side of the yard and quickly cut visibility down to a couple of yards in any direction. Guy felt himself start to cough as the fumes caught in the back of his throat and felt the rope slide between his palms as he fought desperately to keep Camus alive.

A moment later he was aware of a second tremendous crash behind him followed by the unmistakable phut-phut sound of small-calibre fire through suppressors.

A deeper crack, then another and another betrayed the presence of someone else with a pump action tactical shotgun; what the American cops referred to as an "alley cleaner".

A small corner of his brain registered - double taps - professionals at work - before he was wracked again by a coughing fit. His feet in the too large gumboots slipped again and he heard the sound of Camus' screaming cut off abruptly once more as he was dropped back head first into the foul ooze at the bottom of the well.

Two small hands closed around the rope just in front of his own and he blinked back the tears to look at their owner. Almu. She smiled at him for a second then added her weight to his own. With her efforts they again made progress and raised Camus back up once more from certain death.

All around them was utter mayhem. Men were screaming and shouting as their unseen assailants continued to progress and lay waste to their number. It became clear that there had been an attack on the front and rear of Baserri Otxoa simultaneously. An unknown force of what appeared to be professional soldiers had breached the gates while at the same time another group were attacking via the rear entrance, just by where the cells used to be that had housed Guy and Camus.

In their place was now a large and smoking hole in the wall.

More flash-bangs went off front and rear and added to the confusion.

Otxoa was nowhere to be seen, and neither was Joni; both had taken the opportunity to disappear under cover of the smoke. A small group of men, Azkuna among them, had grouped themselves together to one side and were casting about nervously looking for someone or something to shoot at. Elsewhere in the building bursts of automatic fire and single shots were subsiding; the only sound that remained consistent was the rhythmic double-tap of silenced weapons.

Then silence fell; a shocking counterpoint to the previous deafening noise. Beside him, Guy heard Almu whimper and across the courtyard he heard a weak coughing coming from the well. A strong voice rang out from somewhere close by, although he couldn't see the speaker.

'Put down your guns. Hands on your heads. Do it. Kneel down. You are outnumbered and surrounded. Your position is hopeless. Put down your guns and you will live. Do it. Do it now. NOW.'

Eneko Azkuna had never been the brightest of souls. Throughout his short and brutal life he had distinguished himself by poor life choices. This time was no different. He raised his Skorpion machine pistol and deliberately aimed it at the exposed and helpless Guy and Almu. 'YOU surrender. Or they d…'

He never finished the sentence. His last. He never saw or heard the .50 Cal. shell that caught him full in the chest and blasted him back against the courtyard wall. Barratt and Barrett, working in perfect harmony at a muttered command from Andre Lucas. His three companions, dropped their own guns immediately and raised their hands as their friend's blood dripped from their shocked faces. Two heavily armed Royal Marine Commandos emerged from the back of the courtyard and took them into custody.

Guy felt rather than heard the man who suddenly appeared at his side. Two strong hands in tactical gloves grabbed at the rope and started to heave. Two more figures moved swiftly past, towards the well. One, smaller than the other, kept a machine gun at their shoulder and scanned the area constantly for further threats. The second, taller and long-haired, reached down into the well and manhandled Camus back out, lowering him to the ground and cutting his bonds with a couple of swift slashes from a knife at his belt.

Once he was sure that Camus was out of danger he straightened and walked back to where Guy sat exhausted on the ground.

Andre Lucas looked down at the Queen's Wayfarer and smiled. At least he was bringing him back alive. Colour Sergeant Hood dropped the rope he had been holding and offered Guy a drink of water from a canteen. Guy lay back and gulped fresh air then took the proffered canteen and drank deeply.

As the tears cleared from his eyes he saw Almu standing uncertainly a few feet away. The lithe figure he had seen earlier had her covered with what looked like a Diemaco C7. Lucas crouched down beside him and waited for Guy to focus on him. His own combat shotgun was slung over his back. He pushed his long hair back out of his eyes and smiled.

'Taxi for Mr. Miller? Cash only - I'm afraid we don't take credit cards.' To one side he heard the Colour Sergeant snort derisively and mutter "Amateurs."'

Guy grunted and struggled to his feet. Lucas helped him get up and kept a steadying hand on his arm and shoulder as he swayed unsteadily.

Guy started to talk then spluttered and was wracked with another coughing fit. Another swig of water and he tried again.

'Lucas, isn't it? I remember you from London. You run the get-you-home boys, don't you?'

'And girls...' Shepherd chimed in.

Miller nodded with a smile. He pointed at Almu. 'Turns out she's one of the good guys after all. Treat her well.' Then he looked over at where Camus lay, tended by one of the Commandos. 'Is he alright? He's a pain in the arse but...'

'He'll live.' Said Hood. 'He swallowed some of that shit at the bottom of the well but Pierce has given him emetics and an adrenaline shot. A strong course of antibiotics and he'll be fine.' As he spoke Camus suddenly retched onto the ground and coughed a stream of filthy black water.

'He's French secret service. Not to be trusted.'

'We know, Guy. We will deal with him accordingly.' Lucas turned back to Hood. 'Time to go, I think, Colours.'

Hood nodded and led the way back inside through the hall and headed for the front courtyard where they had "parked" their farm truck after battering it through the front gates.

He was first out of the door and the bullet that smashed into his chest knocked him off his feet.

Chapter 33

Lucas, next in line, grabbed Hood's webbing harness and pulled him back into the relative safety of the doorway. He bent over the Colour Sergeant as the other two Marine Commandos took up defensive positions. Behind them, Shepherd covered Almu and Camus. Lucas ran his hands quickly over Hood's chest, trying to assess the damage.

'Off you fuck - Sir.' Lucas stepped back as the Royal Marine struggled back to his feet, wheezing hard. 'Kevlar. Lovely stuff. I'll have a bruise, but no worse than a smack from a squash ball. He grudgingly accepted an arm from Lucas and scrambled back to his feet. The two men assessed the situation.

'We missed one.' Said Lucas.

'Evidently. At least.'

'Gentlemen in the house.' Otxoa. 'My associate and I are ready to leave now. You will not stop us. Your friend - the one you left looking after your transport - is injured but alive. He will remain that way if you grant us safe passage.'

Lucas thumbed his comms button and spoke under his breath. 'Barratt - do you have eyeball?'

'No Sir. I do not.

There are overhanging pantiles, and your own truck slap in the middle of everything. I can't resolve a target.'

Hood had crossed to a window overlooking the front courtyard and was carefully trying to see where Otxoa was speaking from. He pointed.

'I can see a pair of legs. From the boots, it's your man, Romano. He's on the far side of the truck. He's not moving.'

Lucas stiffened. 'I've never lost a man on an extraction, Colours. Today is not the day. Am I clear?'

'Sir.' Hood started to speak again but was interrupted by Almu.

'Let me talk to them. My cousin, Joni is out there. Perhaps I can…'

Lucas held up a hand.

'No. We are not here to negotiate. We are here to extract and depart.' He paused for a moment. 'We don't know how badly Romano's hurt and we don't have time to waste.' He turned back to Hood.

'Did you lock the door after us as we discussed?'

Hood nodded. 'Just in case.'

Lucas stood and moved towards the door, being careful not to expose himself to further fire. He cleared his throat.

'We won't stand in your way. Feel free to fuck off - but leave my man behind so that we can get him medical attention.'

There was a long pause then Otxoa spoke. 'Agreed. Mr. Miller? Are you there?'

Lucas beckoned Guy forward.

'What do you want, Otxoa?'

'I did not want us to part on bad terms. You could have had a much easier stay with us, you know. You are stubborn, Englishman and I respect that.
In another life we could have been allies.'

'In another life I'd have smashed your face in. Fuck off, Otxoa.'

'*Gero arte*, Englishman.'

The sound of a powerful engine being started filled the courtyard. A late model white Toyota Landcruiser pulled out from under cover, driven by Joni. Otxoa was in the front passenger seat.

'Barratt - hold. Let them go.''

'Sir.'

Joni edged the Landcruiser past the bulk of their truck and headed toward the shattered gates. As he did so he wound down the window and shouted.

'Almu - come!'

Miller whirled to where Almu stood. He saw in her face the same fire that he had witnessed when they first met and she was held at knifepoint by Leon Camus. She stepped forward and dodged past Lucas and Hood to stand in the doorway.

'No. Joni. No. Not this time. You are on your own.'

Joni shrugged and smiled a wolfish grin. 'Your choice.' He reached down between his legs and pulled out a dark shape then threw it towards the farmhouse.

'Grenade!' Shouted Lucas, grabbing Almu by the shoulders and pulling her back off her feet to safety. The fragmentation grenade bounced towards the doorway and only stopped moving when it rolled to a halt at the bottom step.

The blast when it came a second later was deafening but those inside were shielded from the shrapnel by the steps. The glass in the window shattered and rained down on them where they crouched for cover. Miller started to rise but Hood waved him down again. 'Wait!'

Under cover of the explosion, Joni gunned the big Landcruiser straight towards the gate. As they passed through they snapped the thin, almost invisible wire that one of Hood's men had strung across the entrance. The two Claymore mines – planted one on each side of the narrow gateway - detonated almost simultaneously, their blast directed towards each other, creating a lethal killing zone.

One thousand four hundred steel ball bearings shredded the Landcruiser into confetti together with the two men inside. The blast, in the confined space, was deafening. The Claymores had been planted by Hood's men as an insurance policy; they could be readily deactivated for their own departure but were meant to protect their rear whilst they were occupied inside - their actual use was unintended, but undeniably effective.

As soon as the smoke cleared Hood, Lucas and one of the Marines ran out to where Romano lay. He had been shielded from the explosion by one of the tyres of their truck and was unharmed beyond the hen's egg sized lump on his head from where Joni had surprised him earlier.

Inside the Baserri Almu sobbed in Guy Miller's arms.

'He was my cousin, Guy! He did not need to die.'

Guy said nothing; there was nothing he could say. He waited until the sobbing subsided then took Almu by the shoulders.

'Almu. Today you lived. This could all have ended very differently.' Behind her, Lucas caught Guy's eye and tapped his watch.

'Time to go. We'll have to leave via the back door now.' He turned to Hood who was already on comms. He looked up and answered Lucas' unspoken question.

'We are regrouping at the rear of the property. We have secured the hostile survivors; they can wait for someone to turn up - which won't be long since we have just made enough racket for a minor war…' His eyes flicked up at the pall of black smoke that was rising from the wrecked Landcruiser. 'We need to not be here.'

Miller looked at Almu - and at Camus, still under the watchful eye and barrel of Beth Shepherd. He was at least standing under his own steam now. 'What about them? We can't leave them here.'

'We can't take them either.' Hood responded flatly. We need to move fast and you are enough of a challenge in that regard.'

'Well excuse me.' Miller retorted. 'You didn't have to come.'

'I did - to keep an eye on this bunch of amateurs.'

There was a crackle from the comms. Lucas listened for a moment then spoke.

'Colours is right. That was Barratt. There's a string of vehicles on the way here on the road from Getaria; blues and twos. Somebody's pissed. He's heading in our direction asap and once he's here we leave.'

They made their way back through the shattered farmhouse in single file. Miller paused in Otxoa's hall. 'Just a minute' he said and stepped across the room to where the desk stood, coming back with a bundle of his clothes and his Billingham bag. 'I'm not bloody leaving this.'

Lucas gave him a knowing look and moved on. As they walked, Shepherd spoke up. 'Sir - how? How do we leave? We came here by boat, which is now stashed just above the shoreline below the N-634. We won't get far in that.'

'I know.' Lucas rummaged in a pocket and pulled out his phone. 'Time to call in just one more favour.'

--o-0-o--

A little over two hours later Flight Lieutenant Booker found himself headed at speed once again towards the Spanish coastline. He had already apologised profusely to the *Salvamento Maritimo* - he had thought his nav was fixed but it seemed he had the same issues as before - so inconvenient, he explained.

He made a case for intersecting the Spanish mainland to get his bearings once and for all and from there, make his way once more back to his waiting ship. Petty Officer Owen sat beside him in the cockpit as the shadows lengthened and watched a small readout in front of him. 'There.' He said. 'Two degrees Starboard, fifteen nautical miles.'

Back on board RFA *Wave Ruler* Lieutenant Bailey had had a similar terse conversation with the Spanish maritime authorities and had patiently explained that they were altering their own course to shorten the distance that their troubled helicopter would have to fly back. The fast fleet tanker was now making speed across the Bay of Biscay towards the same patch of coastline as Booker and Owen. The command to divert had come direct from Northolt; it was exceptional, but orders were orders.

On the shore, Lucas and Hood stood with a small GPS beacon on the ground between them. Two of the Royal Marine Commandos were drying themselves off having taken the Rigid Raider out into deeper waters and scuttling her by means of small explosive charges.

Barratt and the third Marine were keeping watch whilst Shepherd kept an eye on Romano, who was sitting looking pale with a large bandage on his head. He rued the day he had ever met Guy Miller – first a broken nose and now this...

Camus and Almu sat on some rocks, talking to Guy, who was lying with his back against a large boulder and his leg stretched out in front of him. His hands were bandaged and a large dressing was across one side of his face, making it difficult for him to see.

'What now, *Mon Ami*? Are you taking me back to Britain to face charges? I assure you they will not stick. I am simply a tourist, who got mixed up in a mess of your own making.'

Miller smiled thinly. 'I'm given to understand that we genuinely don't have room to take you. There's no alternative but to set you free when we leave. Lucas tells me that you weren't bluffing – but that your little Welsh girlfriend suffered more than somewhat at the hands of my wife when she came calling so at least I don't have to kill you for harming her. As long as I never see you again, you'll be fine.

'I must still thank you for saving my life. If you had not held the rope as you did I would have died.' Camus shuddered. 'Death in a Spanish well - hardly befitting a French gentleman.'

'You deserved it, you fucking bastard.

But I couldn't let a scabby dog drown like that.'

'Camus shrugged. 'I only know of one way to drown, Guy. But thank you anyway. I am in your debt and I will not forget. I will repay you, one day.'

'For what that's worth.' Interjected Almu. She was still in a state of shock from the death of her cousin but had started at least to function again. '

I will report back to the ruling executive of ETA that Otxoa at least will not make trouble again.' She swallowed hard. 'It will be far harder to tell my uncle that he has lost his eldest son.... This one -' she indicated Camus with a jerk of her thumb '- had better stay out of my way too. *Zakila!*' She spat at Camus' feet.

'Always the lady.' Said Camus with a smile, then coughed again. 'Unless you need me any further I will make my way back to the motorway and find a lift. Adieu my friends. It was a grand adventure.'

Camus stood and started to walk away. Shepherd raised her weapon but Miller waved the barrel down. 'He's no threat now. Let him go.' She glanced across at Lucas who, after a moment's thought, nodded.

Guy turned to Almu. 'And what of you? We can't take you either. Where will you go?'

Almu touched his hand and gave it a short squeeze.

'This is my country, Guy. I am at home. Wherever I go I can be sure I will be safe. It will not take me long to get back to my family.'

Colour Sergeant Hood looked out across the sea and up at the Northern sky. 'Incoming.' He said. 'Three minutes.'

Almu knelt beside him on the sand and kissed Guy on the cheek. 'Goodbye. Again. This time for real.' She gave him a hug and then stood back to watch as the Merlin swept in from the sea and touched down a short distance away. Moments later they were headed back to *Wave Ruler* and safety.

Chapter 34

24 hours later, rested and fed, Guy Miller sat in the briefing room aboard *Wave Ruler*. Present were Lucas, Shepherd and Barratt. Colour Sergeant Hood stood to one side near the door, not really a formal part of proceedings but involved nonetheless. Romano was in sickbay under observation; x-rays showed that he had a fractured skull and the medics had ordered that he rest until their next port of call - Gibraltar.

Guy had similarly been checked over and treated for his many cuts and bruises. His knee was heavily strapped and a walking stick was propped by his chair. He had finally stopped aching - mainly due to the cocktail of drugs that had been pumped into him by the ever efficient Royal Navy Medical Officer.

A large flat screen at one end of the room snapped from screen-saver to the face of Roger Bowman. Conversation died and everyone turned in his direction.

'Guy. It's good to see you in one piece.' He began warmly. Guy cut him off.

'No thanks to you and your piss poor rinky dink organisation. You couldn't keep a secret to save your lives - and I damn near lost mine. What the HELL happened, Bowman?

I was intercepted by Inspector Clouseau's evil twin almost immediately, not to mention the bloody Spanish equivalent of the Provisional IRA.'

'Yes, I know. All deeply unfortunate. Turns out we had a mole. Dealt with now though. Largely by your wife, it must be said.'

Guy allowed himself a small smile. The first thing he had done upon boarding *Wave Ruler* was to refuse to move until he was put in contact with Jane Miller. After tearful reassurances that he was in fact alive, well and coming home, she had filled him in on what had happened in her own words.

He was simultaneously horrified and intensely proud of his resourceful - and more than somewhat dangerous - wife.

Bowman's next words brought him back into the room. 'Ah, I hate to ask, but - where is the dispatch? You *do* still have it don't you?' Lucas reached under the table and pulled up Guy's Billingham. He pushed it across towards where Guy sat.

'You were very keen not to leave without this; I assume you have stashed the micro SD card somewhere inside?'

Guy looked slightly taken aback. 'What? No. I mean, I did, for a while, but I transferred it elsewhere way back in the Cathedral in Seville.

I just wasn't going to leave my camera behind.'

He pushed his chair back from the table and kicked off the boot that he had been given. Lifting his leg up he put his foot on the conference table. He then pulled off his sock, to show his bruised and blistered toes.

'Compeed.' He said, picking at the plaster on his big toe. 'Waterproof, very sticky, stays in place until it drops off - or you pull it off.' He managed to get a nail under an edge and to the fascination of all sitting around the table - and Bowman on the big screen - he peeled back a strip of soft plastic to reveal, between two layers of plaster, the unmistakable shape of a small black micro SD card.

'Here's your dispatch.' He said, holding it up so that the camera could see it. He handed it over to an astonished Lucas. 'Over to you for safe keeping. I've had enough.'

--o-0-o--

A week later Guy sat beside Jane Miller on a scheduled flight from Gibraltar back to London Gatwick. On the same flight were Lucas and his team, dispersed among the passengers so as not to draw attention. The micro SD card was inside Lucas' smartphone where it would remain safely until they reached London.

Jane Miller relaxed back in her seat as the seatbelt signs were switched off. She was a nervous flyer and take off from somewhere like Gibraltar was more than somewhat nerve-wracking for her. She let go of Guy's hand and pointed down at the Rock.

'We must come back, Guy. It would be nice to get to see a bit more of the place.'

Guy nodded. 'I'll book something up in a bit - a holiday, not work.'

Jane's face clouded again. 'Are you going to carry on with this lot? The Wayfarers? It's hardly safe, Darling…'

Guy thought long and hard before replying. 'Maybe not as safe as some of the things I've done, Jane, but nothing I have done before has actually mattered quite so much. I had time to think – really think - aboard *Wave Ruler* as we rounded the Iberian Peninsula and I've come to the conclusion that I'm going to carry on - if they'll have me. It was hardly a raging success for a first outing.'

'You came home alive, Guy. That was all I asked.' She pecked him gently on the cheek. '…and anyway, next time I'm coming too.'

Afterword

Leon Camus sat uncomfortably on a gilt chair in a cold corridor of the Élysée and waited. He had been summoned as soon as he had crossed the border into France. He had taken the time to clean up and put on a suit, but he fancied he still smelled of the Spanish well.

A door opened and he was ushered into a large, airy office. He was motioned to sit; another gilt chair; no respite there.

'*Je suis désolé ...*' He began his carefully rehearsed *mea culpa* but was cut short. He listened in astonishment as it was explained to him that far from his career being over and the *Direction Générale des Études et Recherches* being wound up, he was being given increased funding and resources. His lone crusade in Portugal and Spain had, apparently, demonstrated that there was a place in the new world for his particular skills – and patriotism. He left with a spring in his step and a new purpose. Hold the line – at all costs.

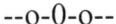

Ruth Owen sat in her cell, rocking gently and counting her blessings. True, she was behind bars, remanded in custody and awaiting a trial date. True, her money had been tracked and frozen. True also that she would likely never walk again without a limp, and would require corrective surgery for months to come. True that she would never see Leon again. But she was prisoner #1 in the just opened HMP Berwyn, the UK's newest, most secure "super prison". In Wrexham... Wrecsam. *Cymru*.

She smiled. She had come home.

--o-0-o--

Andre Lucas looked around the Queen's Wayfarers conference room and glanced down again at his notes. Bowman had been as good as his word and had resigned as soon as Guy Miller had returned to British soil. It had been accepted and he was added to the list for a knighthood in the New Year's Honours – the least that could be done for a loyal servant of The Crown who had given it so much of his life for so long.

It was a shame, he was told, that he was choosing to step down just as the Queen's Wayfarers were moving into a new era of relevance and activity, but it was understood and accepted that he wanted to spend more time with his family.

What Lucas had not expected was the call to come to Sandringham himself. Now just a couple of short weeks later he sat at the round table at the place marked N. It hadn't sunk in yet, but he had busied himself making some immediate organisational changes.

To his left sat Beth Shepherd, newly appointed Head of Field Support. She would lead the team in the Operations Room using her real-world experience to sharpen the way that Wayfarers were tracked and monitored. It had been his most controversial appointment but he had decided that Shepherd had suffered enough for her ill-advised dalliance with Bowman. It was a new start for her and one that he thought she was going to relish.

Near the door to the Ops. Room stood Duncan Hood. His suit was a little too tight and his haircut still made him look like a football hooligan but he was starting to relax into civilian life and had taken to his new role as Head of Safety for the Wayfarers like a duck to water. He'd be fine, Lucas mused, and he could keep Romano and Barrett in line while they sought a replacement for Shepherd.

Opposite Lucas at the South position sat Guy Miller, talking quietly to Linda DiSanto. His bruises had faded but he was still walking stiffly and was glad of the seat.

The doctors had recommended that his knee operation was delayed no further so he was going in to hospital in a couple of days and would then be recuperating in a spa on Gibraltar before resuming his duties as the newest Queen's Wayfarer.

The rest of the room was filled with other Wayfarers and backroom staff standing around in small groups and clutching glasses of warm champagne. The buffet that he had ordered was quietly festering off to one side.

No time like the present, he thought, and got to his feet.

'I'd just like to say a few words,' he began and cleared his throat. 'The Queen's Wayfarers stand today at the start of a new era. We have a job to do unlike any other. We must pass through society unobserved – un-noticed – bearing the burden of information that can – and will – change lives – and governments.'

There was a slight ripple at that; the General Election had been called just days after Miller's dispatch had reached Downing Street.

Lucas raised his hand for silence and continued. 'There's nothing new about what we have to do. But the world in which we do it today has changed beyond anything that could be dreamt of by Frances Walsingham. It is harder than ever to operate off-grid because the very grid itself is everywhere now.

It is harder to travel incognito when our every move is tracked and monitored.' He stole a glance at DiSanto and carried on.

'Our support operations now are more important than ever. That is why I have strengthened our hand in the Ops. Room.' A nod to Beth. 'We must find new and innovative ways for our people to stay safe and to stay below the radar. We must perfect the art of hiding in plain sight once again now that every phone is a high resolution camera and every meal is posted to the internet before a fork is even stuck into a sausage.'

Polite laughter. Lucas waited for it to subside and turned serious again.

'Today, our Wayfarers are one of this country's greatest assets. If knowledge confers power, then information enables insight and as the world changes – for good or ill – the uninformed will lose out. All of us here have a job to do. The realm depends upon us, now more than ever.'

He picked up his own glass and raised it to those present, saving the last nod for Guy Miller, who returned it in kind.

'Let's go to work.'

The Queen's Wayfarers will return soon in a brand new adventure - "Sharp Focus"!

What's real – and what isn't – probably...

This is a work of fiction, however it draws heavily upon the real world in which it is set. The places are all real, as is the political backdrop. All the organisations are real, with the exception of Otxoa's rogue group and of course the Queen's Wayfarers themselves. Even Camus' *Direction Générale des Études et Recherches* existed once, long ago, but no more – I think.

The great thing about writing a book like this is the chance to stretch the boundaries just a little. Westminster was really a royal palace, but there are no secret organisations hiding in the basement – as far as I know. Bowman's globe, of which he is so proud, is close to realisation and makes a nice centrepoint to the Wayfarer's conference room.

Fuji make cameras of course, and the X-Pro2 is very real. I have one, and the possibilities offered by the actual dual SD slot capability was one of the triggers for the book – it offered me the ability to hide something in a way that most people would not suspect. The "firmware upgrade" that enables the camera to be turned into a communication device is fictional, but again, not beyond the bounds of possibility...

All of the military hardware is real, up to and including RFA *Wave Ruler*. I am not, however, aware of her taking part in any clandestine operations in the Bay of Biscay.

The "superprison" in which Ruth Owen finds herself is really just being brought into operation during 2017. It was one of those real-world "coincidences" that enabled me to give a neat ending to Ruth's story arc.

The Queen's Wayfarers operate against a backdrop of massive political, social and technological change. At time of writing the French and British governments are heading to the polls so by the time you read this the world could have changed once again.

I started writing this book (on a beach) last Summer and since then it has sometimes been hard to keep up with events – the election of Donald Trump triggered a mild rewrite...

I hope you've enjoyed reading this book as much as I have writing it. The next Queen's Wayfarers outing – provisionally entitled "Sharp Focus" - is on the way!

Acknowledgements

I'd like to thank my long suffering Wife Becky, who has found herself a veritable book widow at times whilst I spent long hours researching and hammering the keys. Her patience and forbearance meant that I was kept fed and watered while wrestling with such difficult issues as whether or not a Merlin Mk3 or a Merlin Mk2 was the most appropriate form of transport for a clandestine operation into a friendly country.

I'd like to thank the following, without whom this book would never have seen the light of day and whose encouragement, advice, guidance, specialist knowledge and expertise, proofreading skills and general good sense have been invaluable: Rod Carr, Peter Mead, James O'Connell, Mark Parsons and Sippora Veen.

About the Author

Bill Palmer is an experienced writer, photographer and regular traveller who is based in "Sunny Frimley" in Surrey. He has photographed worldwide for over thirty years and describes himself as a "Gentleman Amateur", shooting more for enjoyment than for personal gain.

Today, Bill often creates under the pseudonym "Lightmancer". He is an Associate Editor of the photo and technology website Macfilos.com and a moderator on Serious Compacts and FujiXSpot.

This is his second book. The first, *"F8 and Been There"* is also available on Amazon Kindle. It's a non-fiction, photographer's-eye guide to ten European cities, helping the reader to decide what's worth seeing and what isn't as well as the best kit to use.

You can find more of Bill's photography at Lightmancer.uk and on Instagram.

Printed in Great Britain
by Amazon